Emily McGinnis

P9-CRB-580

Emily McGinnis

The Tale of Genji

A NOTE ON PERSONAL NAMES
Japanese personal names are given surname first, the normal order used in
the Japanese language (e.g., Miyata Masayuki rather than Masayuki Miyata).

Distributed in the United States by Kodansha America, Inc., 575 Lexington
Avenue, New York, N.Y. 10022, and in the United Kingdom and continental
Europe by Kodansha Europe Ltd., 95 Aldwych, London WC2B 4JF.
Published by Kodansha International Ltd., 17-14, Otowa 1-chome, Bunkyo-ku,
Tokyo 112-8652, and Kodansha America, Inc.

ISBN 4-7700-2772-9
First edition, 2001
01 02 03 04 05   10 9 8 7 6 5 4 3 2 1

Chapter summaries by Watanabe Ayako and Hiraoka Michiko
Book design by Point & Line

The Tale of Genji
Scenes from the World's First Novel

by Murasaki Shikibu

宮田雅之 ［切り絵］
Illustrations by Miyata Masayuki

瀬戸内寂聴 ［序文］
Introduction by Setouchi Jakuchō

ドナルド・キーン ［エッセイ］
With an essay by Donald Keene

マック・ホートン ［英訳］
Translation by H. Mack Horton

KODANSHA INTERNATIONAL
Tokyo • New York • London

目次 ◆ CONTENTS

「源氏物語」と絵画

瀬戸内寂聴

　二十世紀最後の夏、沖縄で開かれたサミットを記念して発行された新二千円札には、国宝源氏物語絵巻の「鈴虫」の帖の名場面が採用され、紫式部の肖像まで入っている。

　千年前に紫式部の書いた「源氏物語」は、当時から貴族仲間で愛読され、今ならさしずめベストセラーナンバー１の折紙がつく人気小説であった。

　印刷術のなかった当時は、墨で書かれた原稿を、人々が作者に借りて、筆写して、拡まった。おそらく、写しながら、絵心のある人は必然的に、挿絵のように名場面で絵を描き入れたであろう。また、絵の上手な友だちに描いてもらった絵を綴じこんだのではないだろうか。

　当然、絵の本職は、名場面の絵を依頼されて描いていくうち、それは絵巻物として仕上げられていったであろう。

　この場合、絵が主体になり、文章は説明的に短く付け加えられる場合もあった。

　平安時代、絵画は貴族たちの教養の大切なものの一つと数えられていた。宮廷や高級貴族の間ではお抱えの絵師もあり、名人たちに描かせた屏風絵や襖絵は自慢の一つであった。「源氏物語」の中でも「絵合」の帖があり、華麗な宮中の絵の競争場面が描かれている。

　冷泉帝には権中納言（もとの頭の中将）の娘、弘徽殿の女御が早くから入内していた。そこへ源氏が親代りとなって、六条の御息所の娘、斎宮の女御が入内する。この女御は冷泉帝より、はるかに年長なので、帝は、はじめはなじまず、自分と年の似た弘徽殿の女御に親愛感が強かった。しかし斎宮の女御が絵を描くのが上手だったので、絵の趣味の強い帝は、次第に同じ趣

Painting and *The Tale of Genji*

Setouchi Jakuchō

In the last summer before the year 2000, the Japanese government issued a new two-thousand-yen note commemorating a summit held in Okinawa. Prominent in the design of the new note is a portrait of Murasaki Shikibu, author of *The Tale of Genji*, together with a famous scene from the "Bell Crickets" (*Suzumushi*) chapter of the twelfth-century *The Tale of Genji Picture Scroll*, a National Treasure. The gesture reflects the unflagging popularity of the classic, beloved by its first readers in the Heian court a thousand years ago and still a bestseller today.

In the absence of printing presses, the first readers of Murasaki's masterpiece borrowed the manuscript from the author herself, copied it, and passed it on to their friends at court. Some, as they copied the successive chapters, doubtless added their own illustrations of the most moving scenes, or had such pictures made by artistically inclined friends and inserted them into the text. Professional artists were also commissioned to paint illustrations, and gradually picture scrolls of the tale developed. In such cases, the pictures became the focal point, and the text was abbreviated to the minimum required to explain each scene.

It was natural that the tale was illustrated almost from its inception, given the fact that painting was an important part of the cultural education of Heian aristocrats. The court and the great noble houses also maintained professional painters and took pride in owning artwork that particularly famous masters created on walls and free-standing screens. The competitive nature of art collecting at the time is memorably depicted in the chapter of *The Tale of Genji* entitled "The Picture Contest" (*Eawase*), in which two of the Reizei Emperor's consorts use pictures to vie for his affection. The consort

味の新しい女御に興味と魅力を覚えていく。

　それを見て焦った権中納言は、絵の名人たちに命じて物語絵の傑作を作製して後宮に収め、帝の愛を娘につなぎとめようとする。その結果、二人の女御が、帝と母后の藤壺の宮の御前で左右に分れ、持っている絵を競いあって勝負をすることになる。その場面が「絵合」の帖である。最後は源氏が流謫の地須磨で描いた日記絵によって、斎宮の女御方が勝ちを決めるという話である。

　この場面の絵は、風景画、花鳥、人物画ではなく、物語の一場面を絵画化したものであった。

　時代が下っても、絵描きはこの傑作物語に創作欲を刺激されて、屏風や、絵巻物に描いている。

longer in service, Kokiden (not to be confused with the Kokiden at the beginning of the tale), is the daughter of Genji's friend and rival Tō no Chūjō, a Provisional Major Counselor at the time. The other, Akikonomu, daughter of Genji's late mistress Rokujō and now his ward, is a recent addition to the imperial harem. Akikonomu is considerably older than Emperor Reizei, and he is initially more at ease with Kokiden, who is nearer his age. But Akikonomu is a fine painter, and the Emperor, who loves art, grows gradually more intimate with her. This causes grave concern to Kokiden's father, Tō no Chūjō, and he fills his daughter's rooms with the works by the finest professional artists in order to lure the sovereign back to her. Both factions finally decide to hold a picture competition and pit their finest works of art against each other in the presence of the Emperor and his mother, the Dowager Fujitsubo. The last piece of art shown is an illustrated diary made by Prince Genji while exiled in Suma. It dwarfs the competition and wins the day for his ward, Akikonomu.

The Tale of Genji continued in succeeding centuries to serve as the inspiration for countless screens and picture scrolls.

「源氏物語」の再現

ドナルド・キーン

「源氏物語」は、言うまでもなく日本文学の最高峰である。十一世紀初期にこの物語が書かれた頃からすでにそう評価されてきた。おそらくこの小説の挿絵もまた、作者紫式部がまだ生存中に描かれていたものと思われる。これよりやや遡った時代に書かれた「宇津保物語」の最も古いテキストの中に、「絵解」によって多くの挿絵が描かれていたという記述があるところから、「源氏物語」もこれと同様ではなかったかと思われる。

　昔の日本人にとって、本というものは、ただ単に何頁にもわたって、一連の言葉が綴られているだけのものではなく、その内容に添った美しい筆跡や、物語の随所にほどこされた挿絵を鑑賞する貴重な芸術品でもあった。この、本に対する美意識が、「源氏物語」より数世紀前に、すでに日本人が木版による印刷技術をもっていたにもかかわらず、この物語を十七世紀になるまで印刷をしなかった大きな理由ではないかと考えられる。

　現代人の本に対する意識とは違って、専門的論文や、通俗的な雑誌に使われている活字と同じもので印刷され、たった一葉の挿絵すらない無味乾燥な「源氏物語」の版などは、当時の人々が愛蔵した物語と挿絵の見事な調和から生まれた華麗な芸術品に比べれば、およそほど遠いものであったに違いない。

　これまでに描かれた「源氏物語」の挿絵の中で、最も著名なものは、十二世紀、藤原隆能によって描かれたとされる「源氏物語絵巻」である。一部の専門家は、この絵巻物の華やかな色彩構成と、優美な書体から成る「隆能源氏」を日本芸術の最高傑作であると評価している。もちろん、この絵巻の芸術的価値を、日本の優れた他の芸術、例えば絵画、彫刻、陶芸などと比較して、具体的にその優劣を証明することは難しいにせよ、こ

Depictions of *The Tale of Genji*

Donald Keene

The Tale of Genji is without question the greatest work of Japanese literature. It has been recognized as such almost from the time it was first composed in the early eleventh century. Probably illustrations for the novel were made even while the author, Murasaki Shikibu, was still alive. We know from indications in the oldest text of a some-what earlier novel, *The Tale of the Hollow Tree*, that it originally con-tained numerous illustrations, and the same was likely to have been true of *The Tale of Genji*. For the Japanese of the past, a book did not consist simply of a series of words inscribed on a number of pages; it was also a work of art, enhanced by the beautiful calligraphy and the illustrations inserted at appropriate places in the story. This may be why the Japanese, although they knew the art of printing centuries before *The Tale of Genji*, never printed the work until the seventeenth century. For Japanese of the past an edition of *The Tale of Genji* of the kind people normally read today, printed from type identical to that used in scholarly reports or in popular magazines, without a single illustration, would have seemed a totally inadequate substitute for the magnificent ensemble of text and pictorial beauty to which they were accustomed.

The most celebrated illustrations ever made for *The Tale of Genji* are the horizontal scrolls known as *Genji Monogatari Emaki*, often credited to Fujiwara Takayoshi, a twelfth-century painter. Some experts consider that these scrolls, in brilliant colors and graced with superb calligraphy, are the very finest work of Japanese art. Obviously, there is no way to prove that these scrolls are superior to any other work of painting, sculpture, ceramics, and so on; but it can hardly be doubted that they are masterpieces of the highest order.

The existence of the *Genji Monogatari Emaki* did not discourage

の隆能の源氏が、傑出した力作であることは疑う余地もない。

　藤原隆能の「源氏物語絵巻」の存在は、後世の芸術家の気を
くじくことがなく、むしろ彼らの源氏絵に対する執着を高め、
ある時は依頼者の要請により、または画家自身の創作意欲に
よって「源氏物語」の挿絵を描きたいという望みをこの上もな
く掻き立てた。何世紀にもわたって、膨大な数の挿絵が登場し、
ついには源氏の挿絵だけで成り立つ大規模なコレクションが設
けられるまでに発展した。さらに、挿絵の領域だけにとどまら
ず、絵画、版画、織物、衣装の染模様に至るまで、「源氏物語」
の筆文字の美しさや、代表的場面を表現したすばらしい芸術作
品が生まれた。

　そして今、宮田さんは「源氏物語」に魅せられた画家として
の創意を、彼自身の切り絵(剪画)という独自の技法で再現する
ことで、まったく新しい源氏絵の分野を開拓した。宮田さんが
「源氏物語」の五十四帖を一帖一作ずつの切り絵で仕上げる構
想を考えたのは、きわめて自然のことと思われるが、一度そう
決めてしまうと、この物語の全編に流れている統一したイメー
ジを保ちながら、各帖のもつ特徴を一枚の絵でいかに伝えるか、
どの部分を取り上げて絵にするかという点で、想像を絶する苦
労があったと思う。

　帖によっては、あまりに平調で、絵になりにくいところと、
逆に非常に劇的で挿話にあふれているところがあり、そうした
静と動との異質な可能性を含むこの物語の中から、自分が表現
したい物の対象を抽出していくことが、宮田さんにとっていか
に困難な仕事であったかが分る。

　"若紫"の帖は「源氏物語」全体の中で最も美しい場面の一つ
であるが、一面では実に動きのない、心理的描写の多い帖でも
ある。

　ここで光源氏は十歳の童女、紫の上を垣間見て、自分の手許
で育てる決心をする。また、この帖には主人公の光源氏と、そ
の正妻である葵の上との不穏の兆しも含まれており、同時に、
光源氏とその父帝の后である藤壺との情交によって、藤壺が源

later Japanese artists who at the request of some patron or purely of their own volition desired to illustrate *The Tale of Genji*. Many, many sets of illustrations were executed over the centuries, so many that one could build a considerable art collection that consisted exclusively of such illustrations. Not only are there paintings but woodcuts and even magnificent robes that, though obviously not illustrations in the usual sense, suggest by their patterns and by words from the text woven into the fabric specific scenes of the novel. The *kiri-e* (paper cut-out) illustrations by Miyata Masayuki carry over into still another medium the artist's desire to express in his chosen manner his love for the original work.

It was natural for Mr. Miyata to have chosen to make one *kiri-e* for each of the fifty-four chapters of *The Tale of Genji*, but once this decision was made he had the more difficult task of determining just which scene he would depict in his *kiri-e* in order to convey the prevailing quality of the whole chapter. Some chapters are undramatic and do not lend themselves readily to being illustrated, others are so full of incident that Mr. Miyata probably had trouble choosing among the different possibilities.

The *Wakamurasaki* (Young Lavender) chapter is one of the most beautiful in the entire novel, but it contains little action. This is the chapter in which Genji sees Murasaki, a girl of ten, for the first time and decides he will raise her in his own house. The chapter also contains a tense scene between Genji and his wife Aoi, and it is at this time too that Genji learns that his affair with Fujitsubo, his father's consort, has had the disastrous result of leaving Fujitsubo with child. None of these developments lends itself readily to an illustration, so Mr. Miyata chose another course: he typified the chapter by the central character, the little girl Murasaki, and filled the sky above her with cherry blossoms which, as we are told in the novel, were at their height when Genji first glimpsed Murasaki. It is a breathtakingly beautiful composition which exploits to the full the possibilities of the *kiri-e*.

The *Aoi* (Hollyhock) chapter is an example of a section of the book with almost too much action. This is the chapter in which Lady

氏の子供を産むという悲劇的運命が語られているが、これらは容易に絵にし難い要素ばかりである。宮田さんはそこで、全く別の視点からこの帖をとらえた。

　つまり、幼き日の紫の上を対象に選び、その童女の頭上から空へかかる一面を万朶の櫻で埋めつくした。この櫻花は、物語の伝える通り、光源氏が初めて紫の上を垣間見た時に満開であった。"若紫"の帖は五十四作の源氏絵の中で、特に宮田切り絵の真髄を心憎いまでに駆使した、息をのむほど美しい構図の作品である。

　"葵"はこの物語中、最も劇的な要素の強い帖である。六条御息所の怨霊が葵の上を責め苛み、ついには死に至らしめるというくだりは、能楽「葵の上」でも知られている有名な場面である。しかし、生霊に取り憑かれて苦悶する葵の上や、その怨霊を退散させるための僧たちの加持祈禱の激しさ、あまりの恐怖と悲しみに呆然とする光源氏を含めて、その光景を一枚の絵で現わすことは、もし可能であっても絵が説明的になりすぎて面白くない。この帖で宮田さんは、六条御息所の葵の上に対する憎しみの根源——賀茂神社の祭礼で、彼女の乗物が理不尽にも葵の上の車に押されて後方へ追いやられた時の忍び難い屈辱感——をとらえた。ひしめきあう牛車で賑わう賀茂の祭りの雰囲気を感じさせながら、宮田切り絵の刀の走りから生まれる鋭い線の強さが、牛車のすだれに半身を隠すようにして乗っている女性の悲し気な表情など、その心理を劇的なまでに完璧に伝えきっている。

　宮田さんは「源氏物語」の最も代表的な、そして感動的な瞬間をつかみ取り、それを自らの切り絵の技で、当然あるべきものを産み出すような自然さで、まったく新しい分野の源氏物語を誕生させることに成功した。

　それは、神技ともいえる彼の切り絵によるものだけではなく、宮田さんが日本文学の最高峰である「源氏物語」の深奥までを完璧に読破した、秀れた感性の持主であることの証しでもある。

Rokujō's vengeful spirit torments and finally kills Genji's wife, Aoi. The attempts by priests to exorcise the "living ghost" of Rokujō form the central part of the Nō play *Aoi no Ue*. But it would have been difficult if not impossible to capture the frightening intensity of Aoi in agony, the priests frantically praying, Genji stunned by these developments. Mr. Miyata chose therefore to depict the cause of Rokujō's hatred of Aoi—the humiliation she felt when her carriage was jostled by Aoi's at the Kamo Festival. The thrust of the black lines of the *kiri-e* perfectly conveys the drama of the confrontation of the two women, one of whom can be seen in her carriage, partially obscured by the reed blinds.

Behind each of Mr. Miyata's superb illustrations there is not only the skill of the artist but the sensitivity of a reader of *The Tale of Genji* who has chosen the most typical and most affecting moments of the novel and transformed them into works of art that grow naturally from his chosen medium.

TRANSLATOR'S NOTE

The translation retains the traditional Japanese system of counting age, in which a person is reckoned as one year old at birth. The lunar calendar is retained as well, in which months fall generally four to six weeks after their modern Western counterparts. But whereas characters in the Japanese original are often referred to by office titles that may change from chapter to chapter as they rise in the court bureaucracy, personal names are sometimes simplified and regularized here. Modern Japanese names in the Introduction are given in Japanese order, surname first.

Parts One and Two of "Young Greens" (*Wakana*), which are each normally counted as a separate chapter of the tale, are here combined to allow for the inclusion of a chapter for which only the title remains, "Hidden in the Clouds" (*Kumogakure*).

The relationship between certain chapters and their titles or illustrations may remain opaque in this synopsis, due to limitations of space.

The Tale of Genji

Scenes from the World's First Novel

桐壺（*Kiritsubo*）The Paulownia Court

1 桐壺

　桐壺帝の後宮(宮中の后や女官たちの住まい)に、それほど高い身分でもないのに帝の寵愛を一身に集めている、桐壺の更衣と呼ばれる女性がいました。桐壺の更衣はやがて帝の第二皇子(光源氏)を出産します。しかし、第一皇子(後の朱雀帝)の母である右大臣の娘の弘徽殿の女御など、女御や更衣たちの烈しい嫉妬や憎悪に耐え切れず、身も心も病み、源氏が三歳の時にこの世を去ってしまいます。

　桐壺帝は第二皇子を皇太子にすることも考えましたが、高麗(朝鮮半島にあった国)の人相見の予言に従い、皇位を巡る権力争いに巻き込まれないよう臣下に下ろし、〈源氏〉姓を与えます。皇子は光り輝く美しさから〈光君〉〈光源氏〉と呼ばれるようになりました。

　桐壺の更衣亡き後、悲しみのあまり政務も手につかない帝を心配した臣下は、更衣に瓜二つという先の帝の姫君を后に迎えます。帝の心もようやく癒され、源氏もこの五歳年上の継母である藤壺の宮に亡き母の面影をかさね、慕うようになるのでした。

　源氏は、十二歳で迎えた元服(男子の成人式)の日、左大臣の姫君、葵の上と結婚します。政略結婚でもあり、源氏は四歳年上で気位の高い葵の上になじむことができません。それより、元服後に会えなくなった藤壺への思いがさらに深まり、いつしか恋心へと変わっていくのでした。

The Paulownia Court (*Kiritsubo*)

Among the women in the palace of the Emperor was one named Kiritsubo (Paulownia Court), who though only an Imperial Concubine enjoyed the Emperor's undivided affection. Before long she bore him his second son. Other palace women, especially Junior Consort Kokiden (Palace of Expansive Beauty), daughter of the Minister of the Right and mother of the Crown Prince (the future Emperor Suzaku), were consumed with jealousy, and their ill will sent Kiritsubo into a decline. She passed away when her son was only three.

The sovereign, known as Emperor Kiritsubo, wanted to change the succession in favor of this second son, but in view of an augury by a Korean physiognomist, he instead gave him the name Genji and lowered him to the ranks of the common nobility to protect him from a struggle for the throne. A child of dazzling beauty, he came to be known as "the Shining Prince."

After the death of Kiritsubo, the grief-stricken Emperor was incapable of dealing with affairs of state. Afraid for him, his ministers eventually arranged for him to take another woman as his wife, the daughter of a former sovereign and the very image of the earlier lady. The Emperor's grief left him, and Genji, who was only five years younger than this new stepmother, Fujitsubo (Wisteria Court), began to transfer to her the longing that he had felt for his dead mother.

At age twelve, Genji underwent his coming-of-age ceremony, and on the same day, he was betrothed to Aoi (Hollyhock), daughter of the Minister of the Left. It was a political marriage, and Genji found it impossible to warm to this elegant and reserved woman four years his senior. Instead, his attraction to his stepmother, whom he was unable to see after donning adult dress, continued to deepen to the point of love.

帚木 (*Hahakigi*) The Broom Tree

2 | 帚木

　源氏十七歳、中将の頃のことです。五月雨の続く夜、宮中の宿直所に籠もる源氏が、妻の葵の上の兄弟で親友でもある頭の中将とお互いの恋について話していたところに、左馬の頭、藤式部の丞が訪れ、それぞれが恋愛体験を語りはじめ、女性論が繰り広げられました。「雨夜の品定め」と言われる場面です。

　左馬の頭が話す嫉妬深い妻や浮気な女の話、頭の中将の行方知らずになった女(後に登場する夕顔)の話、藤式部の丞の博学だが女らしくない学者の娘の話など。その中で、源氏は中流階級の女性にこそ思いがけない魅力的な女がいるという話に興味を持ちます。

　翌日、源氏は、左大臣邸に帰りますが、方違え(悪い方角を避けること)のために急きょ左大臣家に親しく仕える紀伊の守の別邸に向かいました。そこには紀伊の守の若い継母の空蟬も来ていました。かつては宮仕えの話もあった空蟬ですが、父衛門の督に死なれて後見(後ろ盾)を失ったため、弟を連れて紀伊の守の父の伊予の介の後妻になったのでした。昨夜の中流階級の女性の話を思い出し、空蟬に興味をもった源氏は、その夜、寝所に忍び込んで強引に関係を結んでしまいます。

　その後も空蟬のことを忘れられない源氏は、空蟬の弟の小君を手なずけて再会の手引きをさせますが、空蟬は自分の身の程を思い、頑なに拒むのでした。

The Broom Tree (*Hahakigi*)

Genji was now seventeen and a Middle Captain. One evening when the court was in ritual seclusion in the long summer rains, he was passing the time chatting about women with his close friend Tō no Chūjō, the brother of his wife Aoi and a Middle Captain as well. As the two talked, Hidari no Umanokami, Director of the Imperial Stables of the Left, and Tō Shikibunojō, a functionary in the Ministry of Rites, happened by and volunteered love anecdotes of their own. A discussion of the merits of various types of women ensued, a scene in the tale now known as "the rainy night conversation."

Hidari no Umanokami spoke of one woman of marked jealousy and another of no less promiscuity; Tō no Chūjō, of a lady (later revealed as Yūgao [Evening Faces]) who suddenly disappeared; and Tō Shikibunojō, of a scholar's daughter as unladylike as she was learned. Genji took particular interest when the talk turned to the surprising charm of some women of the middle ranks of the aristocracy.

The next day he returned to the house of his wife and father-in-law, the Minister of the Left, but due to a directional taboo he subsequently removed to the villa of the Governor of Ki, one the Minister's inner circle. At the villa was the Governor's young stepmother, Utsusemi (Cicada Shell). She had once been considered for court service, but the early death of her father Emon no Kami, Commander of the Gate Guards, left her without the necessary political backing, and so she became the second wife of the Governor of Ki's father, the Vice Governor of Iyo, and brought her younger brother Kogimi to live with them as well. Genji took particular notice of Utsusemi in view of the discussion of middle-class women the previous evening, and later that night he stole into her bedchamber and had his way with her.

Unable to forget her thereafter, Genji tried to arrange another meeting with the help of her younger brother Kogimi, but Utsusemi was well aware of the disparity in their positions in the world and resolutely refused him.

空蟬 （*Utsusemi*） The Cicada Shell

3 | 空蟬

　空蟬を忘れることができない源氏は、紀伊の守の留守中、夏の夕闇に紛れて三度目の中川の邸訪問をしました。偶然、碁を打つ空蟬と紀伊の守の妹である軒端の荻の二人を垣間見（垣のすき間からのぞき見ること）た源氏はやはり、色白で可愛らしい軒端の荻に比べて、不器量ではあるけれども、たしなみ深くて品のある空蟬のほうに魅力を感じるのでした。

　その夜、源氏は小君の手引きで再び空蟬の寝所に忍びこみますが、その気配を察した空蟬は薄衣を残し、寝所を抜け出してしまいます。源氏は、一人残されて寝ていた軒端の荻を空蟬と思いこみ、別人だと気づいた時はすでに遅く、それでも軒端の荻に人違いと悟られないよう取りつくろって、契ってしまうのでした。

　源氏は空蟬の仕打ちを腹立たしく思いますが、空蟬の残していった衣をひそかに持ち帰り、寝るときもその衣を抱いて残り香をなつかしみますが、眠れぬままに、空蟬への思いの丈を歌に詠むのでした。

> 空蟬の身をかへてける木のもとに
> 　　なほ人がらのなつかしきかな
>
> 〈蟬が脱皮した木の下で、抜け殻のような衣だけを残して去ったあの人の人柄が慕わしいことだなあ。〉

　小君が持ち帰ったその歌を見て、空蟬の心は揺れ動きますが、受領（地方官）の後妻という今の立場を考え、やはり源氏の誘いには応じないのでした。そして源氏の歌の隣に、

> 空蟬の羽におく露の木がくれて
> 　　しのびしのびに濡るる袖かな
>
> 〈空蟬の羽に置く露が木の間に隠れているように、私の袖も忍び泣く涙で濡れることですよ。〉

と人知れず書きつけるのでした。

The Cicada Shell (*Utsusemi*)

Infatuated with Utsusemi, Genji went a third time to the Governor of Ki's villa on the Inner River under cover of the dark summer evening. Stealing a glance into the room, Genji chanced to see Utsusemi and the Governor of Ki's younger sister, Nokiba no Ogi (Reeds Beneath the Eaves). Utsusemi was not as pretty as the fair Nokiba no Ogi, but Genji found her cultivation and elegance the more attractive.

That night, he again enlisted the help of Kogimi to sneak into Utsusemi's bedchamber, but sensing his presence Utsusemi made her way out of the room, leaving a thin robe behind. Genji mistook the sleeping Nokiba no Ogi for her, and by the time he discovered his mistake, matters had already gone too far, so he hid his mistake from her and made her his.

Genji was piqued by Utsusemi's behavior, but he nevertheless took home with him the robe she had left behind. He brought it to bed with him, and lying sleepless with the memories its scent brought back, he expressed his longing in verse:

> At the foot of the tree
> where the cicada
> shed its shell,
> how I miss the one
> who left it behind!

Kogimi took the poem back home with him, and Utsusemi, though deeply moved by the sentiment it contained, knew her place as the second wife of a provincial governor, and in the end did not pursue the connection. But unknown to others, she wrote this poem next to his:

> Dew on the wings
> of the locust
> lying hidden neath the trees—
> secret, secret tears
> that wet my sleeves.

29

夕顔 (*Yūgao*) Evening Faces

4 夕顔

　源氏は、その頃通っていた六条の高貴な女（後に登場する六条の御息所）を訪ねる途中、五条に住む病気の乳母を見舞いに寄りました。乳母の家の門が開くのを待っていた源氏は、隣家の垣根に咲く白い夕顔の花が目にとまり、一房所望します。その家の女童（召使いの少女）は、香をたきしめた白い扇に夕顔の花を載せて持ってきました。その扇には歌が書かれていました。

心あてにそれかとぞ見る白露の
ひかりそへたる夕顔の花

〈もしや光源氏の君かしらと想像しています。白露の光が添えられてひときわ美しい夕顔の花のように、光り輝くお顔は。〉

　源氏は、思わせぶりなその歌に心そそられ、乳母の息子である従者惟光に、隣家の様子を探らせますと、そこには若い女が隠れ住んでいることが分かりました。源氏は身分を明かさないまま、その女（夕顔）のところに通うようになります。

　八月十五夜、夕顔邸を訪れた源氏は明け方近く、夕顔を近くの廃院に連れ出します。二人きりの楽しい時を過ごしていましたが、次の日の夜、夕顔は突然物の怪に襲われ息絶えてしまったのです。源氏は悲しみにうちひしがれ、ついには病に倒れるほどでした。

　後日、源氏は、夕顔の侍女の右近から、夕顔が頭の中将の忍び通っていた人で、頭の中将の妻の実家から脅迫されたため、中将との間にできた女児を連れて隠れ住んでいたことを聞き、その女児（後の玉鬘）の世話をしたいと申し出るのでした。

Evening Faces (*Yūgao*)

On the way to the home of an elegant lady he was seeing in the Sixth Ward (Rokujō), Genji made a detour to the Fifth Ward to pay a sick call on his old nurse. While waiting for the door to open, he noticed white "evening faces" blossoming on the fence next door and asked for one. A serving girl brought one out to him on a scented white fan on which was written this verse:

↳ scent = attraction

> Might it be
> who one thinks?
> An evening face
> made more radiant
> by the dew!

The coquettish verse aroused Genji's curiosity, and subsequent inquiries by his man Koremitsu, the son of his nurse, indicated that a young woman, Yūgao, was living there in seclusion. Without revealing his identity, Genji started to visit her.

Near dawn on the night of the full moon of the eighth month, Genji took Yūgao to an empty villa where they could enjoy being alone together. But that night she was suddenly possessed by an evil spirit and died. Horrified, Genji fell ill himself.

He later discovered from Yūgao's lady-in-waiting Ukon that the dead lady had once been the lover of Tō no Chūjō. Pressured by the family of Tō no Chūjō's principal wife, she had gone into seclusion with their daughter. Genji thereupon offered to provide for the child (the future Tamakazura).

若紫（*Wakamurasaki*）Young Lavender

5 若紫

　十八歳の春、瘧病（おこり）にかかった源氏は、病気回復の祈禱を受けるため北山に出かけました。夕暮れ、寺からほど近い、ある僧都の庵を垣間見ていた源氏は、尼君の側で、雀に逃げられて泣いている少女に目を奪われます。その少女は源氏が恋慕ってやまない藤壺にあまりにもよく似ていたのです。

　僧都に少女の素性を聞き出し、少女若紫（後の紫の上）が藤壺の姪だと知った源氏は、自分の手で理想の女性に育てあげたいと思い、引き取りたいと申し出るのですが本気にされません。

　源氏は都に帰り、妻葵の上を訪ねますが、あき足りなさを感じていました。

　その頃、藤壺は病のため宮中から里下がりしていました。このことを知った源氏は、藤壺の侍女の王命婦に手引きをせがんで寝所に忍びこみ、ついに一夜を共にしました。藤壺はその結果、懐妊してしまいます。

　しばらくして、北山から帰京した少女若紫は、祖母の尼君が亡くなり、疎遠だった父兵部卿の宮邸へ引き取られることになりました。これを知った源氏は、父親の迎えが来る前夜、ひそかに少女を自分の邸に連れてきてしまいます。源氏は永遠の女性藤壺を思い描きながら、少女若紫を大切に育てるのでした。

Young Lavender (*Wakamurasaki*)

In the spring of his eighteenth year, Genji suffered an attack of chills and fever, and he went to a mountain temple to solicit prayers for his recovery. That evening he chanced to look through the fence of the cottage of a bishop nearby and caught sight of a child weeping by the side of her nurse over her lost sparrow. The child (Murasaki) bore an astonishing likeness to Fujitsubo, with whom Genji was still in love.

Asking the bishop about the girl's family, Genji found that she was in fact Fujitsubo's niece, and he was then and there taken by the notion of raising her to be his ideal woman. But his request to bring her back with him was not taken seriously.

Genji subsequently returned to the capital, but when he visited his wife Aoi he could not help but feel deflated.

Fujitsubo, meanwhile, had gone home from the palace to recover from an illness. Genji discovered this, and with the aid of her lady-in-waiting Ōmyōbu, he stole into her bedchamber and finally spent a night with her.

Some time later, little Murasaki came back from the Northern Hills. Due to the death of her cloistered grandmother, it was decided that she should move into the mansion of her hitherto estranged father, Prince Hyōbu, the Minister of War. Genji found out, and the night before she was to go, he spirited her away to his own residence. Though his longing for Fujitsubo continued unabated, he began to oversee little Murasaki's upbringing.

Murasaki looks like Fujitsubo
Fujitsubo = beautiful
So ...
M = beautiful too!

末摘花（*Suetsumuhana*）The Safflower

6 | 末摘花

　源氏ははかなく亡くなってしまった夕顔のことが忘れられず、あのような心休まる女性はほかにいないものかと思い、探し続けていました。

　そんなある日、源氏は、乳母子(乳母の実子)の命婦(後宮の女官)から、故常陸の宮の姫君が、宮の死後、ただ琴だけを友にしてひっそりと暮していることを聞きました。興味をもった源氏は、春の月の美しい夜、命婦の手引きで常陸の宮邸を訪れ、ひそかに姫君の琴の音を聞きます。その帰り道、源氏を尾けていた親友の頭の中将に姫君の存在を知られてしまい、以来二人は競争するかのように姫君に恋文を送るのでした。

　その後いくら待っても、二人共に姫君から返事は来ません。業を煮やした源氏は命婦に手引きを催促し、八月二十日過ぎ、忍んで宮邸を訪れ、ついに姫君と結ばれました。ところが、姫君のあまりにも世間知らずな様子に失望します。落胆して帰った源氏は、後朝の手紙(共寝した翌朝、男から女に贈る手紙)を夕方になってようやく出すのでした。

　その後、行幸(天皇が外出すること)の準備で多忙なこともあって、足も遠のきました。

　雪の降る夜、久しぶりに源氏は姫君を訪れましたが、翌朝の雪明かりに、姫君の鼻が象のように長く、鼻先が紅花(末摘花)のように赤いのを見て、あまりの不器量さに失望するのでした。

　しかし源氏は、亡き父常陸の宮の家を守り続ける末摘花に同情し、生活面の援助は続けようと決意するのでした。

The Safflower (*Suetsumuhana*)

Genji still found his lost Yūgao impossible to forget, and he continued to look for another who could put him so much at ease.

Then one day he heard from Myōbu, a court lady-in-waiting and the child of another of his old nurses, that the daughter of the late Prince Hitachi had been living in seclusion since her father's death, with no friend but her *koto*. Seized with curiosity, he went with Myōbu to her mansion one moonlit spring night and secretly listened to the late Prince's daughter play. Unknown to Genji, he had been followed by his friend Tō no Chūjō, who now knew of the lady as well, and they thereafter both wrote letters to her, rivals for her affections.

But wait as they would, the lady answered neither. Vexed, Genji enlisted Myōbu's help and later that month went in secret once more to her mansion and slept with her, only to be later discouraged by her artlessness and naiveté. He returned home disappointed, and it was fully evening before he could bring himself to send her the obligatory "morning-after" note.

Thereafter he was kept away, in part because of preparations for an imperial progress.

Then one snowy night, he paid a long overdue call on Princess Suetsumuhana, and the next morning, in the bright sunlight reflected off the fallen snow, he was put off by his discovery that the tip of her absurdly long nose was as red as a safflower.

And yet he continued to feel pity for this woman who had maintained the late Prince's household, and he resolved to make sure she was provided for thereafter.

紅葉賀（*Momiji no ga*）The Fall Foliage Celebration

7 | 紅葉賀

　源氏十八歳の十月十日過ぎ、朱雀院（上皇）への行幸が計画されました。桐壺帝は、行幸を見ることのできない懐妊中の藤壺のために、清涼殿で試楽（予行演習）を催しました。源氏と頭の中将は青海波を舞い、その美しさに人々は感嘆せずにはいられません。ただ藤壺だけは、帝の寵愛を受けながら、源氏の子を宿しているという身がつらく、素直に感嘆にひたれないのでした。

　産み月は十二月と思われていましたが、翌年二月、予定日から大幅に遅れて藤壺は皇子（後の冷泉帝）を出産しました。世間では物の怪のせいだと取り沙汰していましたが、源氏はやはり自分の子と確信するのでした。産まれた皇子は恐ろしいほど源氏に似ており、藤壺の苦悩は増すばかりでした。

　四月になり、参内した皇子を抱いて喜ぶ帝は、源氏に似ていると嬉しげに見せるので、源氏も罪の大きさに恐れおののくのでした。

　心乱れる源氏にとって、無邪気な紫の上の存在が救いであり、いっしょに過ごす時間が多くなって、いっそう正妻の葵の上との仲は冷めていくばかりでした。

　その頃、源氏は色好みの老女、源の典侍と戯れの恋をします。二人の奇妙な関係を聞きつけた頭の中将も、典侍と通じ、ある時、源氏と頭の中将は典侍の局で鉢合わせをしてしまうという事件がありました。

　七月、帝はこの皇子を皇太子にと考え、藤壺を中宮に、源氏を宰相に引き上げます。それにつけても弘徽殿の女御の不満はつのるばかりでした。

The Fall Foliage Celebration (*Momiji no ga*)

Toward the middle of the tenth month in Genji's eighteenth year, planning began for an imperial excursion to the Suzaku Palace of the Retired Emperor. Since Fujitsubo was with child and unable to see the procession, the Kiritsubo Emperor arranged for her to see a rehearsal at the Seiryōden Palace. The beauty and grace with which Genji and Tō no Chūjō danced "Waves of the Blue Sea" was met with unalloyed admiration by all save Fujitsubo who, beloved of the Emperor but carrying Genji's child, was assailed by very conflicting emotions.

Though expected in the twelfth month, the child (the future Emperor Reizei) did not arrive until the second month of the next year. Spirit possession was widely believed to be the cause, but the discrepancy confirmed Genji's suspicions about his own involvement. The baby resembled his father to an alarming degree, which only increased Fujitsubo's fears.

And when the Emperor first held the child in his arms at the palace in the fourth month, he happily remarked on the similarity, filling Genji with dread at the enormity of his sin.

Only the presence of the innocent little Murasaki relieved some of his inner turmoil, and he spent more and more time with her, which further alienated his principal wife Aoi.

And yet he was still able to amuse himself with a half-hearted courtship of Gen no Naishinosuke, a lady well on in years but still susceptible to male charms. Hearing of the odd liaison, Tō no Chūjō became involved as well, and at one point Genji and he had a mock set-to in her apartments.

In the seventh month, the Emperor decided to make the child the Crown Prince, to raise Fujitsubo from the rank of Junior Consort to Empress, and also to make Genji a Consultant. Kokiden's anger only increased as a result.

花宴（*Hana no en*）The Cherry Blossom Banquet

8 花　宴
はなの　えん

　源氏二十歳の春、宮中の南殿で桜の花の宴が催されました。
宴が終わり、酔心地の源氏は藤壺の局のあたりを窺い歩きます
が、戸は用心深く閉ざされていました。
　何気なく向かい側の弘徽殿の細殿に行くと、戸が開いている
ので、源氏は忍び入りました。そこへ若い身分の高そうな女が
廊下の向こうから、

朧月夜に似るものぞなき
おぼろづき　よ

〈朧月夜ほど美しいものはありません。〉

※朧月夜が口ずさんだ古歌。「照りもせず曇りもはてぬ春の夜の
朧月夜にしくものぞなき」(『大江千里集』)の下の句を、「しく」
おおえのちさと
が漢文訓読語であることから、女性らしく「似る」に言い換えて
口ずさんだものといわれています。

と歌を口ずさみながら歩いてきます。
　源氏はとっさに女の袖を捕らえ、抱きおろしてしまいます。
初めはおびえていた女も、相手が源氏とわかると身も心もゆる
してしまうのでした。契りを交わした二人は、夜明け方、逢瀬
の証拠に扇を交換してあわただしく別れました。
　その後、女の素性を探らせた源氏は、女が右大臣の娘、つま
り自分を憎む弘徽殿の女御の妹らしいことを知り、困惑します。
　　　　　　　　　　にょうご
　女との再会の手だてがなく、思いあぐねて過ぎた一ヵ月後、
右大臣家の藤の花の宴に招かれた源氏は、扇の持ち主を探しま
す。酔ったふりをして姫君たちのいる寝殿に近づくと、ため息
をつく女がいます。もしやと思い、源氏が歌を詠みかけると、
返歌をするその声は、まさに扇を交換して別れた朧月夜の君で
した。
　実は、朧月夜の君は、源氏の兄の東宮(後の朱雀帝)に入内が
　　　　　　　　　　　　　　　　　　　すざく　　じゅだい
予定されていたのでした。

The Cherry Blossom Banquet (*Hana no en*)

In the spring of Genji's twentieth year, a cherry blossom banquet was held in the Grand Hall of the palace. Feeling the effects of the wine after the banquet was over, he went out toward Fujitsubo's apartments, but the door was locked. He then wandered in the direction of the corridor of Kokiden's apartments across the way, and finding the door open, snuck in.

Coming his way from across the corridor was a young and elegant lady who was reciting the second half of a poem that went, " . . . there is nothing like the misty moon." It was a variation on the old verse in the *Ōe no Chisato* collection that goes:

> Neither brightly shining
> nor completely
> obscured—
> there is nothing to compare
> with the misty moon of springtime!

In an instant he took her by the sleeve and drew her down in his embrace. At first alarmed, the lady then recognized Genji and gave herself to him. Afterward, they traded fans as mementos, and then at dawn bade each other a hurried farewell. His later inquiries revealed the shocking fact that she apparently was a daughter of the Minister of the Right and the younger sister of Junior Consort Kokiden, his nemesis.

After passing an anxious month unable to see the lady again, Genji was invited to a wisteria banquet at the mansion of the Minister of the Right, whereupon he sought out the owner of the fan. Pretending to have drunk too much, he worked his way toward the bedchamber of the ladies of the house, where he heard one heave a sigh. Thinking he was in luck, he recited a poem, and the voice that answered with a poetic response was none other than the lady of the misty moon, Oborozukiyo, who was scheduled to enter the service of Genji's elder half-brother, the Crown Prince (the future Emperor Suzaku), son of Kokiden.

葵 (*Aoi*) Hollyhock

9 葵
あおい

　桐壺帝が位を譲り、弘徽殿の女御が産んだ東宮が即位して
（朱雀帝）、藤壺の皇子（後の冷泉帝）が東宮になり、源氏はその
後見役になりました。

　新しい伊勢の斎宮（伊勢神宮に仕える未婚の皇女）には六条の
御息所の娘が選ばれました。源氏の冷たい態度に耐えかねてい
る御息所は、娘と一緒に伊勢へ下向しようかと思い悩んでいま
す。

　賀茂の新斎院の御禊の日、源氏もお供なさるというので、懐
妊中の正妻の葵の上も女房たちにせがまれて、夫の晴姿の見物
に出かけました。六条の御息所も、つれない恋人だけれど、そ
の晴姿を見ずにはいられません。

　一条大路は立錐の余地もないほど、大勢の人々で賑わってい
ました。すでに牛車を止める場所がなく、左大臣家（葵の上の
実家）の権力を笠に着た家来たちは、車争いをし、六条の御息
所の牛車に乱暴して、隅に追いやってしまいました。屈辱を受
けた御息所は、葵の上への憎しみを一気につのらせていきます。

　その後、出産間近な葵の上は、物の怪に取り憑かれてひどく
苦しみ、源氏は何度となく物の怪退散の加持祈禱を行わせます。
ある時、祈禱をさせていた源氏は、六条の御息所の生霊と対面
してしまい、それ以来、御息所が一層うとましくなり、ますま
す心が離れていきます。

　葵の上は無事男子（夕霧）を出産しますが、急な発作でこの世
を去ってしまいます。

　四十九日の喪が明け、二条院に戻った源氏は、久しぶりに見
た若紫（紫の上）がすっかり大人びていることを感じ、新枕（初
めて共寝すること）を交わすのでした。

Hollyhock (*Aoi*)

Emperor Kiritsubo retired in favor of the son of Junior Consort Kokiden, at which point Fujitsubo's son (the future Emperor Reizei) became Crown Prince, with Genji as his guardian.

A new Ise Virgin was also selected, the daughter of Rokujō. Unable to bear Genji's continued coldness, Rokujō disconsolately wondered whether to accompany her daughter to her new duties at Ise Shrine.

On the day of the purification ceremony for the Kamo Priestess, also newly appointed at the start of the new reign, Genji was one of those scheduled to take part. His principal wife Aoi was pregnant, and yet, urged on by her ladies-in-waiting, she went out to see her husband in his finery. And despite his treatment of her, Rokujō, too, found it impossible not to go out and watch him pass by.

Ichijō Avenue was thronged with spectators packed cheek by jowl, and places to park carriages were in short supply. Aoi's retainers, emboldened by the power of their master, the Minister of the Left, forced Rokujō's carriage into a corner to make way for their own lady's conveyance. Her resentment of Aoi was instantly spurred to even greater proportions by this public humiliation.

Near the time of her delivery, Aoi was possessed by an evil spirit and began to suffer cruelly. Genji had any number of prayers and rituals performed to exorcise it, and it finally revealed itself to him as that of the tormented Lady Rokujō. This further alienated him from her thereafter.

Lady Aoi gave birth to a son, Yūgiri (Evening Mist), but then suffered a sudden seizure and died. After the mourning period of forty-nine days ended, Genji returned to his Nijō Mansion. There he saw Murasaki for the first time in a long while. Realizing she was now a young woman, he made her his wife.

賢木（*Sakaki*）The Sacred Tree

10 | 賢木

　六条の御息所は源氏との仲に絶望し、娘の斎宮と共に伊勢へ下ることを決意しました。出発が間近にせまった九月初め、源氏は嵯峨の野宮に籠る御息所を訪れて歌を交わし、別れを惜しみます。

　かねてから病に臥せていた源氏の父の桐壺院は重態となり、長男の朱雀帝に東宮と源氏を重んじるようにと遺言して、崩御されました。桐壺院の弟、桃園式部卿の宮の娘である朝顔が、新しく賀茂の斎院になりました。

　年が明け、権勢は朱雀帝の外戚である右大臣方に移り、源氏や藤壺は次第に圧迫されていきます。そんな中、尚侍（天皇に近侍する内侍司の長官）として朱雀帝の後宮に入った朧月夜の君は、朱雀帝の寵愛を受けつつ、なおも源氏と密会を重ねていました。

　桐壺院の死後、東宮（藤壺の子で、後の冷泉帝）の後見役でもある源氏を唯一の頼みとしていた藤壺でしたが、いっそう迫ってくる源氏を振り切るため、一周忌の法要の後、突然出家するのでした。

　翌年、左大臣が辞職、源氏や頭の中将も不遇の身となります。そんな状況の中、病気のため里帰りしていた朧月夜とひそかに逢瀬を重ねていた源氏は、ある日、激しい雷雨で帰りそびれていたところを右大臣（朧月夜の父）に発見されてしまいます。激怒した帝の母である弘徽殿の大后（朧月夜の姉）は、これを口実に源氏を失脚させようとたくらむのでした。

The Sacred Tree (*Sakaki*)

Despairing of her relationship with Genji, Rokujō finally made the decision to accompany her daughter, the new Ise Virgin, to Ise Shrine. As the date of her departure in the early ninth month approached, Genji called at Nonomiya (Shrine in the Fields) in Saga, where the ladies were staying, and exchanged poetry to mark the parting.

His father the Kiritsubo Emperor had long been in poor health. Now, feeling the end was near, he left instructions to his eldest son, Emperor Suzaku, to give his support to the Crown Prince and Genji. He passed away soon thereafter. Asagao (Morning Glory), the daughter of his younger brother, Prince Momozono, the Minister of Rites, was selected as the new Kamo Priestess.

The new year arrived and with it, new power for the faction of the Minister of the Right, the maternal relatives of Emperor Suzaku. Genji and Fujitsubo found themselves increasingly oppressed. Meanwhile, Genji continued his illicit affair with Oborozukiyo, despite the fact that she was a Principal Handmaid in the service of Suzaku and enjoying his personal favor.

Bereft of the late Kiritsubo Emperor's support, Fujitsubo now had no one to look to for protection but Genji, who was also the guardian of her child (the future Emperor Reizei). But his increasingly ardent advances were also a threat, and so to keep him at arm's length, on the first anniversary of the old Emperor's death, she suddenly took holy orders.

The following year the Minister of the Left retired, placing both his son Tō no Chūjō and son-in-law Genji at a disadvantage at court. Genji nevertheless continued his trysts with Oborozukiyo even after she left the palace due to an indisposition. Finally one day, detained at her house by a violent thunderstorm, he was discovered by her father, the Minister of the Right. Her sister Kokiden, now the Empress Dowager, was furious and then and there resolved to find a way to use this infidelity as a pretext to destroy Genji.

花散里（*Hanachirusato*）The Village of Falling Orange Blossoms

11 | 花散里
はな ちる さと

　源氏は、この世にほとほと厭気がさしているのですが、出家
までは決心がつかないという日々を送っていました。

　そんな中、桐壺院の女御であった麗景殿の妹の花散里のこと
をふと思い出し、五月雨の晴れ間、久しぶりに訪ねることにし
ました。宮中ではかない逢瀬を交わしたことのある花散里は、
院亡き後、姉の女御とひっそり暮らしており、源氏は何かと庇
護しているのでした。

　女御の邸へ向かう途中、中川のあたりで、見覚えのある家に
さしかかります。奥からは美しい琴の音が聞こえ、門の内を覗
き見ると、青葉の匂いが伝わってきます。そこは以前一度だけ
通ったことのある女の家であったと思い出しました。素通りし
て行くのをためらっていたその時、ほととぎすが空を鳴き渡る
声に誘われて、源氏は歌を届けますが、女からはそしらぬふり
をされるだけでした。

　ひっそりとした麗景殿の女御の邸に着き、源氏は女御と桐壺
院の思い出を語り合った後、同邸に住む花散里を訪れるのでし
た。

The Village of Falling Orange Blossoms (*Hanachirusato*)

Genji was daily more discouraged by the turn his life had taken, but he could not yet resolve to abandon the world and take holy orders. In the midst of this depression, he one day recalled Hanachirusato (Village of Falling Orange Blossoms), the younger sister of Junior Consort Reikeiden (Beautiful Vista Palace), one of the ladies of the late Emperor Kiritsubo. During a lull in the summer rains, Genji decided to pay an overdue call. He had had a brief romantic encounter with her while she was serving in the palace, and after the death of his father she had gone to live quietly with her elder sister Reikeiden, receiving some support from Genji.

On the way to Reikeiden's mansion, he chanced upon a house by the Inner River that seemed familiar. From inside came the sound of exquisite *koto* music, and when he peered through the gate, he was greeted by the smell of green leaves. Then he remembered—he had visited a lady here once. He was disinclined to pass by in silence, and as he hesitated a cuckoo flew by, singing. Inspired by its song, Genji sent in a poem, but the woman sent a noncommittal reply.

Arriving later at Reikeiden's quiet residence, he passed some time with her talking of the late Emperor, then called on Hanachirusato.

— Koto music piqued interest
    CDShows attraction / appreciation for
— art important in lifestyle

須磨　Suma

12 | 須磨

　源氏は、政治的に追い込まれていくのを感じ、このままでは後見を任されている東宮の地位も危ういと考え、自ら須磨へ退去することを決意します。

　出発前、源氏は息子の夕霧がいる左大臣家や花散里のところへ挨拶にいき、朧月夜の君には手紙を、藤壺の宮には御簾越しの対面をして別れを惜しみました。特に紫の上を京に残していくことは心残りでしたが、謹慎の身として連れて行くわけにはいかず、泣く泣く別れ、三月下旬、源氏はわずかばかりの供を連れて須磨に出発したのでした。

　須磨の生活のわびしさは想像以上で、都から訪れる人もなく、かつて親交のあった人々との手紙のやりとりだけが唯一、心の慰めでした。

　須磨にほど近い明石に住む入道は、かねがね娘を高貴な人と結婚させたいと思っていました。そこへ源氏の須磨住まいの噂を聞き、これこそ前世の因縁と喜びます。

　今や政局を握る弘徽殿の大后の目を憚れて、都からの便りも途絶えがちでしたが、年が明けて、宰相（もとの頭の中将）が源氏を見舞いに訪れ、束の間の再会を喜び合いました。

　三月、源氏が海岸で御禊をしていると、突然、大暴風雨が襲ってきました。源氏は、この海辺の住まいに堪えられないと思うのでした。

Suma

Genji was being pushed further and further into a corner politically. Realizing that any further erosion in his position would compromise his promise to protect the Crown Prince, he resolved to remove himself from the political arena for a time and go to the seaside village of Suma.

Before leaving, he went to see his son Yūgiri, who was living in the home of the former Minister of the Left. Next, he visited Hanachirusato, and wrote to Oborozukiyo. Finally, he called on Empress Fujitsubo and spoke to her through the blinds about his sadness at parting. He was particularly unhappy to leave Murasaki behind, but as this was a journey of penitence, he could not take her with him, and so at the end of the third month, with only the minimum number of retainers, he set out in tears from the capital.

Life in Suma proved even more lonely and rustic than he had imagined. No one from the capital visited, and letters from old friends were his only consolation.

But nearby in Akashi lived a lay monk who for years had cherished the hope of marrying his daughter to a nobleman, and hearing rumors of Genji's presence in Suma, he rejoiced to think his good fortune must have been the result of some karmic bond from a former life.

As the months passed, even some of Genji's friends in the capital wrote less and less, afraid of the watchful eyes of the politically powerful Empress Dowager Kokiden. But when the new year arrived, Tō no Chūjō, now a Consultant, nevertheless came to call, bringing Genji a glad moment.

In the third month, a year after his departure, Genji went to the seaside for a purification ceremony. When a violent storm suddenly blew up, Genji felt he could endure his rustic seacoast exile no longer.

明石　Akashi

13 | 明石

　暴風雨は何日も続き、源氏の安否を心配する紫の上からの使者によると、都でも天候の異変が続いているといいます。

　嵐がようやくおさまった夜、源氏の夢枕に亡き父桐壺院が現れ、須磨の地を去るようにと告げます。翌朝、同じく住吉の神の夢のお告げを受けて迎えに来たという明石の入道の舟に乗って、源氏は明石へ移りました。

　明石の入道はもともと都人でしたが、変わり者で、地方官になってから、都には戻らず明石に住み着いてしまったのです。入道は一人娘（明石の君）に、最高の教育をして高貴な人と結婚させることを悲願としていました。源氏は入道からその娘のことを聞かされ、娘に恋文を送りますが、娘は身分不相応だと考え、ためらいがちなのでした。

　一方、都では凶事が続き、朱雀帝（源氏の異母兄）は、夢の中で故桐壺院に睨まれてから、眼病に苦しんでいました。太政大臣（もとの右大臣）も亡くなり、弘徽殿の大后も病気がちになるなど、不幸が続いていました。

　八月十三日の月の美しい夜、源氏は入道の岡辺の家に明石の君を訪れ、入道の取りなしもあってついに二人は結ばれました。都で待つ紫の上にはそれとなく手紙で打ち明けました。

　年が明け、譲位を考える朱雀帝は、弘徽殿の大后の反対を押しきって、源氏を都に呼び戻します。源氏は身重になった明石の君を残して、二年数ヵ月ぶりに帰京したのでした。

Akashi

The storm raged for days. Afraid for Genji's safety, Murasaki sent a messenger who told him of similar strange weather in the capital.

The night the wind finally abated, Genji had a dream in which his late father, the Emperor Kiritsubo, directed him to leave Suma. The very next morning he boarded a boat for Akashi sent by the lay monk there. He, too, was acting on instructions vouchsafed him in a dream—his, from the gods of Sumiyoshi.

The monk had originally come from the capital as Governor. An eccentric, he had decided to take up permanent residence in Akashi. But he still hoped against hope for a good marriage for his daughter (later known as the Akashi Lady) and gave her the best possible education. He spoke of her to Genji, who made a tentative overture in a letter. But she hesitated to respond, conscious of the disparity in their social stations.

Calamities continued meanwhile to plague the capital, culminating in a dream in which Genji's elder half-brother, Emperor Suzaku, was glared at by their father and developed an eye ailment as a result. The Chancellor (the former Minister of the Right and father of Empress Dowager Kokiden) passed away as well, and his daughter too suffered from illness.

On the evening of the thirteenth of the eighth month, under a beautiful nearly full moon, Genji visited the Akashi Lady at the hillside retreat of the lay monk, whose efforts were in part responsible for the betrothal that resulted. Genji sent a letter to Murasaki in the capital gently hinting at the news.

The arrival of the new year brought Emperor Suzaku thoughts of abdication, and over the protests of his mother the Empress Dowager, he summoned Genji back. Leaving his pregnant new wife temporarily behind in Akashi, Genji returned to the capital after an absence of two years.

澪標（*Miotsukushi*） Channel Markers

14 澪標

　帰京した源氏は、まず、故桐壺院の追善供養を営みました。
　翌年春、朱雀帝が退位し、冷泉帝(源氏と藤壺の不義の子)が即位しました。源氏も内大臣になり、宰相の中将(かつての頭の中将)は権中納言に昇進します。一方、明石の君に姫君(後の明石の中宮)が誕生しました。
　源氏はその昔、帝・后・大臣となる子を持つであろうという予言をされたことを思い出し、将来后になる可能性のある明石の姫君の養育に心を配ります。
　藤壺は女院(准太上天皇)となり、権中納言の娘が冷泉帝の後宮(弘徽殿)に入りました。
　秋、源氏は住吉にお礼参りの参詣をします。偶然にもその日、住吉に来合わせていた明石の君が、源氏一行の華々しさに圧倒され、参詣を取り止めて引き返したことを知った源氏は、従者惟光に託して明石の君に歌を送りました。
　六条の御息所は、御代代わりで斎宮を解任された娘と共に帰京してきましたが、やがて病気のため出家し、見舞いに来た源氏に、娘の前斎宮(後の梅壺の女御、秋好中宮)の後見を託し、しかしくれぐれも好色の相手にはしないようにと切にお願いし、世を去りました。
　かねてから前斎宮に心を寄せていた朱雀院が、御所に迎えたいと望むのを無視し、源氏は藤壺と相談し、冷泉帝への入内を計画するのでした。

Channel Markers (*Miotsukushi*)

Immediately after returning to the capital, Genji held requiem ceremonies for his father, the late Emperor Kiritsubo. The following spring, Emperor Suzaku abdicated in favor of Reizei, the illicit son of Genji and Fujitsubo. Genji himself was elevated to the office of Palace Minister, Tō no Chūjō was raised from Consultant to Provisional Middle Counselor, and the Akashi Lady gave birth to a daughter (the future Akashi Empress). Mindful of the prophecy that he would one day be the father of an emperor, an empress, and a great minister, Genji set about raising his daughter with that possibility in mind.

Fujitsubo, also, was promoted to the rank of Imperial Lady and awarded emoluments equivalent to those of a retired emperor, and Tō no Chūjō's daughter went to the Kokiden Palace to serve Emperor Reizei.

That autumn, Genji made a pilgrimage of thanks to Sumiyoshi. By coincidence, the Akashi Lady arrived at the shrine on the same day, but intimidated by Genji's grand retinue, she cut short her visit. Discovering what had taken place, Genji wrote her a poem and had his man Koremitsu deliver it.

The change in reigns also brought the appointment of a new Ise Virgin, and Rokujō returned to the capital with her daughter. She fell ill soon thereafter and took holy orders. When Genji went to visit, she commended her daughter (later known as Junior Consort Umetsubo and then as Empress Akikonomu) to him, entreating him not to take romantic advantage of her. She passed away soon afterward.

Despite the fact that Emperor Suzaku had long had his eye on the girl and wanted to take her into his service, Genji decided after a discussion with Fujitsubo to send her into the service of their son Reizei instead.

蓬生（*Yomogiu*）Overgrown Grasses

15 蓬生
よもぎ う

　源氏が須磨・明石で暮らしていた間、末摘花（故常陸の宮の
姫君）は源氏の帰りをひたすら待ち続け、生活は窮乏を極めて
いました。もとより荒れていた邸は雑草が生い茂り、ますます
荒廃して、女房たちも次々去っていき、兄の禅師が時折訪ねる
だけでした。

　末摘花の叔母は、かつて受領（地方官）の妻になったことで、
宮家から軽蔑されたことをひがみ、末摘花を自分の娘の侍女と
して、夫の赴任先に連れていこうとします。ところが末摘花は、
頑として邸を離れようとせず、一途に源氏の再訪を信じて待ち
続けていました。

　源氏は都に戻った翌年、花散里を訪ねる途中、偶然に故常陸
の宮の邸の前を通りかかり、大きな松に藤の花がかかっている
のを見て、ようやく末摘花のことを思い出しました。

　邸内に足を踏み入れると、蓬がひどく茂り荒れ果てていまし
た。自分を信じて待っていた末摘花に心うたれた源氏は、再び
生活の面倒を見ることを誓うのでした。それからは邸内も整え
られ、二年後、末摘花は源氏の二条院の東の院に引き取られる
のでした。

Overgrown Grasses (*Yomogiu*)

Throughout the time Genji had been away in Suma and Akashi, Princess Suetsumuhana, daughter of the late Prince Hitachi, had awaited his return, even as she sank further and further into poverty. Her mansion, never in the best repair, became overgrown with grasses, and as life became more and more straitened, her ladies one by one left her service. Only her elder brother, a monk, paid her the occasional call.

Her aunt was married to a former provincial governor, and smarting under the condescension of her more highly placed relatives, she decided to go with him to his new place of appointment and take Suetsumuhana along as a lady-in-waiting to her daughter. But Suetsumuhana resolutely refused to leave, sure that one day Genji would come back for her.

The year after Genji returned to the capital, he set out to call on Hana-chirusato, and on the way he happened to pass the mansion of the late Prince Hitachi. Noticing the wisteria clinging to the branches of a great pine, he suddenly remembered Suetsumuhana, the Prince's daughter.

On entering, he found the grounds overgrown and dilapidated in the extreme. Moved that she would go on waiting for him in such a place, he renewed his resolve to look after her thereafter and had the mansion repaired, then two years later he installed her in the East Lodge of his Nijō Mansion.

関屋（*Sekiya*）The Gatehouse

16 関 屋

　空蟬は、夫の伊予の介が常陸の介になったのに従って、任地へ同行していました。源氏の須磨退去のことも風の便りに聞いていましたが、便りをするつてはありませんでした。

　源氏が帰京した翌年、任期を終えた夫と共に空蟬は京に戻ってくることになりました。その帰京の途中、逢坂の関にさしかかった空蟬一行は、偶然にも石山詣でに行く源氏一行と出会います。

　源氏はその昔、空蟬との橋渡しをしてくれた、今は右衛門の佐となっている空蟬の弟（かつての小君）を介して、空蟬に文を送りました。空蟬は当時を思い出し、胸にこみあげる思いを、

行くと来とせきとめがたき涙をや
　　　絶えぬ清水と人は見るらむ

〈逢坂の関を往来する人を止められないように、堰き止めかねる私の涙を、絶えず湧き出る清水のようだと、人は見ることでしょうか。〉

と心ひそかに歌に詠むのでした。

　その後、年の離れていた夫が病で亡くなり、空蟬は、継子の河内の守（かつての紀伊の守）がしきりに言い寄るのを厭って、人知れず尼になるのでした。

The Gatehouse (*Sekiya*)

When Utsusemi's husband, the Vice Governor of Iyo, was given a new appointment as Vice Governor of Hitachi, she accompanied him to his provincial post. She had heard rumors of Genji's exile to Suma but had had no opportunity to write.

The year after Genji returned from Suma, Utsusemi's husband finished his term of appointment, and he and his wife went back to the capital. On the way, at Ōsaka Gate, they chanced to encounter the retinue of Genji, who was making a pilgrimage to Ishiyama Temple.

Through his old go-between Kogimi, Utsusemi's younger brother and now an officer of the guards, Genji sent a letter to her. Memories of the past arose in her breast, and she recited this to herself:

> These tears
> when I left and when I returned,
> impossible to hold back—
> do people take them
> for the gate's unquenchable spring?

Some time later Utsusemi's husband, a much older man, succumbed to illness, and Utsusemi, spurning the entreaties of her stepson, the Governor of Kawachi (formerly the Governor of Ki), quietly became a nun.

絵合（*Eawase*）The Picture Contest

17 | 絵合

　故六条の御息所の娘、前斎宮は、藤壺の女院の勧めで冷泉帝に入内することになりました。朱雀院は残念がりますが、入内当日は、豪華な品物を贈ってお祝いをするのでした。

　前斎宮は梅壺の女御(後の秋好中宮)と呼ばれ、先に入内していた権中納言(かつての頭の中将)の娘、弘徽殿の女御と帝の寵愛を競うようになります。

　絵画を好む冷泉帝が、梅壺の女御の画才を認め、ご一緒に絵を描いたり眺めたりして楽しまれることが多くなりました。帝の心が傾きはじめたのを察知した弘徽殿の女御の父である権中納言が、帝の関心を引き戻すために、一流の絵師を集めて描かせた絵を献上するうちに、双方の女御方対抗の絵合の話が持ちあがりました。

　三月、藤壺の女院の御前で絵合が行われましたが、接戦となり、勝負は、帝の御前での絵合に持ち越されました。

　その日は、藤壺、梅壺の女御の養父である源氏、権中納言も同席し、蛍兵部卿の宮(源氏の異母弟)が判者になりました。今回も優劣つけがたい絵が揃い、なかなか勝敗がつきませんでしたが、最後に、源氏の須磨での絵日記が出されました。それは見る者すべての心を打つもので、梅壺の女御方の勝利を導いたのでした。

The Picture Contest (*Eawase*)

Genji's ward, the former Ise Virgin (daughter of the late Rokujō), entered the service of Emperor Reizei on the recommendation of Imperial Lady Fujitsubo. Suzaku was disappointed, but on the day of her installation, he sent lavish gifts.

Now known as Junior Consort Umetsubo (Plum Court, later Empress Akikonomu), she competed for the Emperor's favor with Junior Consort Kokiden, daughter of Provisional Middle Counselor Tō no Chūjō.

The art-loving Reizei recognized Umetsubo's skill at painting, and they more and more often took to looking at pictures together or painting them themselves. Realizing that his daughter, Junior Consort Kokiden, was in danger of losing the Emperor's favor, Tō no Chūjō resolved to recover influence for her by assembling the finest artists and sending their works to the palace. This led to plans for a picture contest between the salons of the two consorts.

A preliminary match took place in the third month in the presence of Imperial Lady Fujitsubo, but the final competition was held in the presence of the Emperor himself.

The fathers of both consorts were present on the day of the final competition, with Genji's younger brother Prince Hotaru (Firefly), the Minister of War, as the judge. As in the preliminary contest, paintings of equal magnificence were displayed one after the next, making it impossible to choose a winner. But at the very end, Genji's own painted diary of his days in exile in Suma was unveiled. It had a stunning impact on all present and won the day for Umetsubo's side.

- appreciation for arts & talents
  ↳ respect for
- Shown throughout. here - painting
  - fund to be   earlier - girl w/ koto
    attractive
    (dismissively
    appreciation)
- Genji paints himself →reveals self through
  - needs for living

松風（*Matsukaze*）The Wind in the Pines

18 松風

　源氏は、自邸二条院に東の院を造営し、西の対に花散里を迎え入れ、東の対には明石の君を住まわせようと考えていました。しかし、明石の君は低い身分を思うと、なかなか上京の決心がつきません。

　そこで、明石の君の父である入道は、嵯峨の大堰に持っていた山荘を修理し、明石の君と姫君（後の明石の中宮）、そして妻の尼君を住まわせることにしました。明石にひとり残る入道との今生の別れを覚悟して、三人は上京しました。

　源氏は紫の上に気兼ねして、なかなか大堰を訪問することができないのですが、造営中の嵯峨の御堂を見に行くことを口実にして、大堰を訪れました。三歳になっているわが娘の姫君に初めて対面した源氏は、思っていた以上に美しく品格のある姫君の将来を考え、二条院に引き取って養育することを考えます。

　予定を過ぎて二条院へ帰った源氏は、明石の姫君を養女として引き取ることを紫の上に相談します。紫の上は、明石の君の存在に、内心おだやかではありませんでしたが、子ども好きの性格なので、姫君を育てることには心ひかれるのでした。

The Wind in the Pines (*Matsukaze*)

Genji finished the East Lodge of his Nijō Mansion. In the west wing he installed Hanachirusato, and the east wing he planned for the Akashi Lady. But the latter was sensitive about her relatively low position in the aristocracy and could not seem to resolve to move to the capital.

Her father, the lay monk, thereupon refurbished a country estate he had at Ōi, in Saga, just west of the capital, and moved her there along with her daughter (the future Akashi Empress) and her mother, now a nun. The three left for the capital, knowing that this was likely a final parting with the lay monk, who remained behind in Akashi.

Out of consideration for Murasaki's feelings, Genji found it hard to visit the Akashi Lady in Ōi, but he finally set out, using a building project nearby as an excuse. Upon seeing his daughter, now three, for the first time, Genji was struck by the little one's beauty and grace, and in view of her likely future, he resolved to bring her to Nijō and have her raised there.

After his tardy return to Nijō, Genji explained the situation to Murasaki and discussed the possibility of her raising the child. Though privately concerned about Genji's relationship with the mother, she liked children and was attracted to the idea of bringing up the little girl herself.

— motherly instinct

薄雲（*Usugumo*）　A Wisp of Cloud

19 薄雲

冬になり、源氏に明石の姫君を引き取る話を聞かされた明石の君は、悩み抜いた末、姫君の将来を考えて娘を手放すことを決心しました。

雪の降る日、源氏が迎えに来ました。姫君は母とともに牛車に乗るものとばかり思っています。明石の君はただただ源氏を信じて、涙にくれながら姫君を渡すのでした。姫君は二条院に紫の上の養女として迎えられました。

年が明け、凶兆を示す天変地異が多発し、太政大臣(葵の上の父)が逝去しました。三月には、女の大厄にあたる三十七歳の藤壺の女院も、病に勝てず崩御(女院が亡くなること)しました。源氏は人知れず深い悲しみにくれるのでした。

夏、冷泉帝は護持僧から、母藤壺と源氏の関係を打ち明けられ、自分の出生の秘密を知ります。驚愕した帝は、実の父を臣下として扱ってきた不孝の罪に恐れおののき、今の天変地異も考え合わせ、源氏に譲位をほのめかします。源氏はこれを固辞し、帝を強く諫めたものの、帝の様子から出生の秘密の漏れたことを感じ取るのでした。

秋、源氏は二条院に里帰りした梅壺の女御と故六条の御息所の思い出を語り、春秋の優劣について論を交わします。梅壺の女御は、母御息所の亡くなった季節である秋が好ましいと答えるのでした(後に秋好中宮と呼びならわされるようになる)。

A Wisp of Cloud (*Usugumo*)

That winter, Genji told the Akashi Lady of his plans for their child. Anguished by the separation, but aware that it was better for the little girl's future, she agreed to let her go.

One snowy day Genji came for the child. When she got into the carriage, she expected her mother to get in with them, but the Akashi Lady gave her to her father, trusting his judgment but weeping nonetheless. It was as Murasaki's foster daughter that she arrived at the Nijō Mansion.

The new year brought with it natural calamities that boded ill, and indeed Aoi's father, who had been promoted from his office as Minister of the Left to Chancellor, passed away. It was also Imperial Lady Fujitsubo's thirty-seventh year, one particularly dangerous for women. Indeed, she, too, fell ill and died, leaving Genji with a deep grief that he shared with no one.

That summer, Emperor Reizei discovered the secret of his birth from an old bishop. Dumbstruck, the Emperor was distraught by his unfilial conduct in treating Genji, his own father, as a mere courtier. This, plus the recent natural anomalies, prompted him to suggest retiring in Genji's favor. His father adamantly refused and recalled his son to his imperial duty, but from Reizei's demeanor, Genji suspected that he had discovered the secret of his birth.

That autumn, Genji shared memories of the late Rokujō with her daughter, Junior Consort Umetsubo, who was currently on leave from court service and staying at the Nijō Mansion. Their discussion led to a debate on the relative beauties of spring and autumn. The lady expressed her partiality to autumn, the season in which her mother had passed away (she later became known as Akikonomu, the Empress who "adores autumn").

朝顔 (*Asagao*) The Morning Glory

20 | 朝　顔

　故桐壺院の弟の一人、桃園式部卿の宮の娘である朝顔の姫宮は、父の死の服喪により賀茂の斎院の職を退き、叔母の女五の宮と一緒に桃園邸に住んでいました。この姫宮に以前から思いを寄せていた源氏は、女五の宮の見舞いにかこつけて桃園邸を訪れます。

　女五の宮は源氏と朝顔の姫宮の結婚を願っていましたが、長年の恋慕の情を訴える源氏に対して、姫宮は一向になびく気配もありません。気持ちのおさまらないまま帰邸した源氏は、朝顔の花に添えて歌を贈るのですが、姫宮は返歌をするだけの、つれない態度をとるのでした。

　世間では、朝顔の姫宮のことを源氏の正妻としてふさわしい身分の方だと噂し、これを耳にした紫の上は、我が身の程を思うにつけても、嘆き煩悶するのでした。

　雪の日、源氏は二条院の童女たちに雪転がしをさせました。その日の夕暮れ、源氏は紫の上に、故藤壺の宮や朝顔の前斎院、朧月夜、明石の君、花散里の人柄について語りました。するとその夜、源氏の夢に藤壺の宮が現れ、話題にしたことへの怨みを述べるのです。源氏は藤壺が成仏するよう、供養をするのでした。

The Morning Glory (*Asagao*)

Princess Asagao (Morning Glory), daughter of Prince Momozono, the Minister of Rites (a younger brother of Emperor Kiritsubo), relinquished her position as Kamo Priestess when she went into mourning upon her father's death. She lived with her aunt, the Fifth Princess, in the Momozono Mansion. Genji had long had his eye on her and went to visit under the pretext of paying a sick call on the Fifth Princess.

The Fifth Princess for her part was hoping for a marriage between Genji and Asagao, but Asagao showed no sign of giving in to Genji despite his protestations that he had loved her for years. He returned home with his feelings still in turmoil and sent her a verse with some morning glories, but her poem in reply was not encouraging.

Gossip held, however, that Asagao was of a station that would well suit her to be Genji's principal wife, and when such rumors reached Murasaki's ears, she tormented herself with fears about her own position.

One winter day, Genji sent the servant girls at Nijō out to play in the snow. That evening he talked with Murasaki about the characters of the late Empress Fujitsubo, the former Priestess Kamo, Asagao, Oborozukiyo, the Akashi Lady, and Hanachirusato. That night Fujitsubo appeared to him in a dream and reproached him for making her a topic of conversation. Genji thereafter had prayers said for her afterlife.

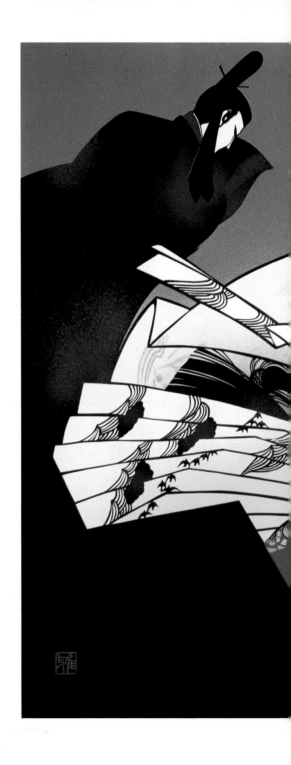

乙女（*Otome*）The Maiden

21 乙女

　年が明け、藤壺の宮の一周忌が過ぎ、朝顔の前斎院も父宮の服喪を終えました。源氏は朝顔への思いを断ち切れず、歌を贈りますが、頑なな態度を変えてはくれません。

　祖母の大宮に預けられていた、源氏と亡き葵の上との子である夕霧は、十二歳で元服を迎え、源氏の邸に移りました。源氏の教育方針により、本来ならば四位に叙せられるところを、あえて六位にとどめ、大学で勉学に専念させることにしました。祖母大宮は源氏の厳しい方針に不満をおぼえます。

　その頃、梅壺の女御が中宮になり、源氏は太政大臣に、かつての頭の中将も内大臣に昇進しました。娘の弘徽殿の女御の立后がかなわなかった内大臣は、次女雲居の雁に東宮入内の期待をかけます。しかし雲居の雁は、同じ祖母のもとで育った夕霧と相愛の仲になっており、これを知った内大臣は激怒して、二人の仲を割きます。

　冬、雲居の雁と逢うことの出来ない夕霧は、五節の舞姫になった惟光の娘を見初めて歌を贈ります。

　源氏は夕霧の後見を花散里に頼みました。夕霧は、それほど美しいとも思えない花散里を、なぜ源氏が長年面倒を見続けているのだろうと不思議に思いますが、花散里の気だてのやさしさを知り、納得するのでした。夕霧は勉学に励み、秋には五位に昇り、侍従となりました。

　源氏がかねてから構想していた、四季の町から成る六条院が完成しました。春の御殿は紫の上、夏の御殿は花散里が住み、秋の御殿は梅壺の中宮(秋好中宮)の里邸とされ、冬の御殿には明石の君が迎えられました。

　秋、里下がりした秋好中宮は、紫の上に紅葉を贈って、秋の美しさを歌に託すのでした。

The Maiden (*Otome*)

The new year came and with it the first anniversary of Fujitsubo's death and an end to Asagao's mourning period for her father. Genji was still attracted to her and sent her another poem, but she stubbornly continued to avoid committing herself.

Genji's son by the late Aoi, Yūgiri, had been in the care of his grandmother, Princess Ōmiya, but after his coming-of-age ceremony at twelve, the young man moved to his father's Nijō Mansion. Genji was a strict parent, and though the son of a man of his stature would normally have been assigned the fourth rank, Genji saw to it that Yūgiri began court life at the sixth and sent him to the university to concentrate on his studies. Ōmiya found Genji's approach hard to accept.

At about the same time, Genji's ward, Junior Consort Umetsubo, was made Empress, and Genji himself was appointed Chancellor. His old friend and rival Tō no Chūjō became Palace Minister. Foiled in his attempt to have his own daughter, Junior Consort Kokiden, made Empress, Tō no Chūjō now placed his hopes on having his second daughter Kumoi no Kari (Goose in the Clouds) installed in the palace of the Crown Prince. But like Yūgiri, she had been raised in the home of her grandmother, Princess Ōmiya, and the two young cousins were in love. Her father was livid when he found out, and he separated them.

Unable to see Kumoi no Kari, Yūgiri that winter took notice of the daughter of Genji's man Koremitsu, who had been selected as a Gosechi dancer, and he sent poetry to her.

Genji had asked Hanachirusato to look out for the boy. Yūgiri had been unable to fathom why his father had continued his association with Hanachirusato after all those years, her looks being nothing out of the ordinary, but now he recognized her kindness and understood what his father saw in her. He devoted himself to his studies and that autumn was promoted to the fifth rank and made a gentleman-in-waiting.

It was also at this time that Genji realized his cherished desire to finish his new Rokujō Mansion, named for its location in the Sixth Ward. Each quadrant was named after a season; Murasaki was assigned to Spring, Hanachirusato to Summer, Empress Akikonomu to Autumn when she was home from court, and the Akashi Lady to Winter.

That autumn, Akikonomu came back from the palace and sent Murasaki some colored leaves along with a poem in praise of the autumn season.

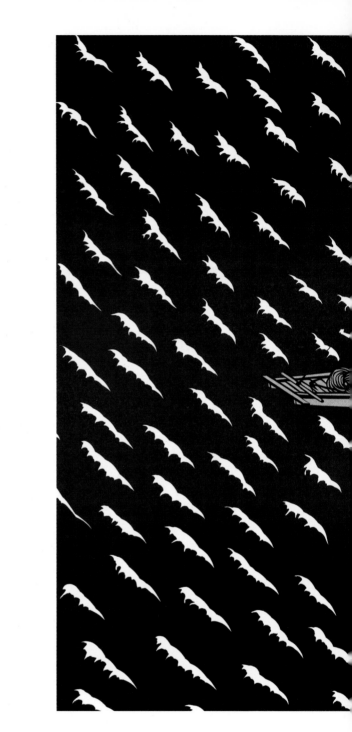

玉鬘 (*Tamakazura*) The Jeweled Garland

22 | 玉鬘

　源氏は、あのはかなく死んでしまった夕顔のことをまだ忘れていませんでした。今は紫の上に仕える、夕顔の侍女だった右近も、もし、夕顔が生きていたら、明石の君くらいの扱いを受けていただろうなどと、何かにつけて夕顔を思い出しています。

　夕顔の遺児の玉鬘は、四歳の時、夫が大宰の少弐となった乳母一家に伴われて筑紫（福岡）へ下っていました。少弐は玉鬘を帰京させるよう遺言して亡くなります。美しく成人した玉鬘に、求婚者は後を絶ちませんでしたが、その中のひとり、肥後（熊本）の有力者である大夫の監が強引に結婚を迫ります。少弐の次男と三男は、地元の有力者との結婚に賛成しますが、長男の豊後の介は、父の遺言を守って筑紫脱出を決意し、乳母と玉鬘の帰京を果たしたのでした。

　京にたどり着いたものの、何のつてもなく途方に暮れた玉鬘一行は、開運祈願のため初瀬詣でに向かいます。そこで、姫君との再会を祈願するため、度々初瀬参りをしていた右近と偶然にも泊まり合わせ、感動の再会を果たしたのでした。

　その報告を受けた源氏は喜び、玉鬘を養女として引き取ることにし、花散里に後見を依頼し、六条院の夏の町の西の対に住まわせました。

　この年の暮れ、源氏は紫の上とともに、六条院の女君たちに、正月用の晴れ着を、ひとりひとりの容貌や性格を思い浮かべながら見立てて贈るのでした。

The Jeweled Garland (*Tamakazura*)

Genji had never forgotten Yūgao's pathetic death. Her old nurse Ukon, now in the service of Murasaki, likewise remembered her at every turn, thinking that had she lived, her late mistress would have received at least the same favor as the Akashi Lady.

Yūgao's daughter Tamakazura, at four years old, had gone to Kyūshū with her nurse, whose husband had been appointed Deputy Viceroy. The husband later passed away after leaving instructions that Tamakazura be sent back to the capital. Now a beautiful young woman, she had no end of suitors, and one of them, a wealthy potentate from Higo (Kumamoto Prefecture) known as Taifu no Gen, tried to win her hand by force. The second and third sons of the late Deputy Viceroy approved of a connection to a powerful local, but the eldest son, the Vice Governor of Bungo, resolved to honor his father's will, and he succeeded in bringing Tamakazura and her nurse, his mother, back to the capital.

After their long journey, they found themselves at loose ends in the capital and went to Hatsuse Temple to pray for direction and good fortune. Ukon, too, had often gone to the same temple to pray that she might meet again with the daughter of her late mistress. They encountered each other at the temple and had a moving reunion.

Genji rejoiced to hear Ukon's news, and he decided to make Tamakazura his foster daughter. He asked Hanachirusato to take responsibility for her and moved her into the west wing of the Summer Quarter of his Rokujō Mansion.

At the end of the year, Genji and Murasaki selected New Year's costumes for the women of the household, matching each garment with the face and personality of the wearer.

— robes represent one's
personality → self expression

初音（*Hatsune*）The First Warbler

23 | 初音

　六条院は、はじめての新年を迎えました。元日の夕方、源氏は、まるでこの世の極楽のような風情の春の御殿で、紫の上と至福の時を慶ぶ歌を交わした後、年末に晴れ着を贈った女君たちをひとりひとり訪れます。

　まず明石の姫君の部屋へ行くと、生母の明石の君から、

> 年月をまつにひかれて経る人に
> 　　今日鶯の初音きかせよ
>
> 〈長い年月を、小松であるあなたにお会いする日を待って過ごす私に、この日の今日こそ、鶯の初音のような言葉を聞かせておくれ。〉

という歌と贈り物が届いていました。源氏は姫君に返歌を書かせます。姫君は、

> ひきわかれ年は経れども鶯の
> 　　巣だちし松の根をわすれめや
>
> 〈お別れして年月は経ちましたけれど、私という鶯は、松の根のように待ち続けるお母様を忘れることなどありましょうか。〉

と詠みました。

　続けて縹色（薄藍）の着物を着た花散里、山吹襲（表は朽葉、裏は紅梅）の晴れ着が美しい玉鬘を訪れて新年の挨拶を交わし、その日は明石の君のもとに泊まります。明石の君は白い着物を品よく着こなしていました。

　二日は、臨時客の華やかな祝宴があり、玉鬘の噂を聞いた若い貴族たちが集まってきました。

　新年の忙しい日々が過ぎてから、源氏は二条の東の院に住む末摘花と空蝉の尼君を訪ねます。

　正月十四日、男踏歌が六条院に廻ってきました。女君たちは南の御殿に集まって見物します。そこで玉鬘は初めて明石の姫君や紫の上と挨拶を交わしました。

　源氏は女君たちを集めて、女楽（女性による管絃の会）を催したいと思いたつのでした。

The First Warbler (*Hatsune*)

The Rokujō Mansion greeted its first spring. On the evening of New Year's day, which this year fell on the first Day of the Rat, Genji exchanged poems with Murasaki in her Spring Quarter, resplendent as a paradise on earth, expressing their perfect happiness. He then called in turn on each woman who had received his present of New Year's robes.

He visited first the suite of the Akashi Princess, and while he was there, gifts arrived from her mother, the Akashi Lady, together with this verse:

> Pining over the months and years
> is this aged one;
> upon this first Day of the Rat,
> let me hear a first note
> from the warbler!

Genji pressed the Princess to reply, and she composed this:

> Though it has been years
> since it departed,
> could the warbler ever forget
> the root of the pine
> where it first left the nest?

Next he called on Hanachirusato, to whom he had presented a robe of light indigo, and then on Tamakazura, who had received a mallow rose combination of russet over plum. He passed the night with the Akashi Lady, who wore her new white robe with elegant perfection. *[handwritten: ex/ of connection of robes to demeanor behavior or personality quali/ies]*

The next day there was a banquet at the mansion, and it was thronged with young men who had heard rumors of Tamakazura.

When the hectic first days of the new year were over, Genji called on Suetsumuhana in the East Lodge of the Nijō Mansion and on the nun Utsusemi.

On the fourteenth, a troupe of male courtiers came to Rokujō for their annual song-and-dance performance, and the women gathered in the main hall to watch. There, Tamakazura met the Akashi Princess and Murasaki for the first time.

Now surrounded by his women, Genji decided that they, too, should stage a concert.

[handwritten: ✶ sing/dancing (performing) = way to show off as well as demonstrate honor, greatness — like Genji's parades earlier]

109

胡蝶（*Kochō*）Butterflies

24 | 胡蝶

　三月、花盛りの六条院の春の御殿で、源氏は竜頭鷁首の船を浮かべて船楽を催し、人々は夜を徹して愉しみました。

　翌日は、里帰りしていた秋好中宮の春の御読経の法会の初日で、人々はそのまま中宮の御殿に参上します。紫の上からは、鳥と蝶の衣装をつけた女童たちを使いにして供花と、去年の秋、中宮と交わした春秋優劣論を意識した歌が届けられてきました。

　夏、次第に洗練されて、美しさを増していく玉鬘のもとに、次々に恋文が届くようになります。源氏は、異母弟の蛍兵部卿の宮や、玉鬘を実の姉と知るはずのない、内大臣の子息の柏木、鬚黒の右大将などからの手紙を見て批評しながら、自らも玉鬘への恋心をつのらせていくのでした。

　源氏を親として信頼しきっている玉鬘は、源氏の気持ちに全く気が付きません。しかし、察しのいい紫の上に感づかれ、源氏は反省するものの、思いを抑えることはできず、ある雨上がりの月夜、玉鬘に添い寝し、意中を告白するのでした。

　玉鬘は思いも寄らない事態に困惑し、苦悩の日々が始まります。

Butterflies (*Kochō*)

[handwritten annotation: Culture of the desire to please/impress others]

When the cherry blossoms of the Rokujō Mansion were at their height in the third month, Genji held a concert on board boats with dragon or fishhawk prows, and his guests spent the night enjoying themselves.

The next day was the beginning of the spring sutra readings of Empress Akikonomu, who was in residence at the Rokujō Mansion at the time. Murasaki sent floral offerings, delivered by girls wearing bird or butterfly costumes. She added a poem composed in the spirit of the spring-and-autumn debate that she had had with the Empress the year before. *[handwritten annotation: poems = friendship here, not courtship!]*

That summer, love letters began arriving thick and fast for Tamakazura, who was growing more elegant and lovely by the day. Genji read and critiqued those of his younger half-brother Prince Hotaru, General Higekuro (Blackbeard), and Kashiwagi (Oak Tree), son of Palace Minister Tō no Chūjō. Kashiwagi did not know Tamakazura was actually his elder half-sister. And Genji began to find himself attracted to her as well.

Trusting him as a parent, Tamakazura did not notice this change in Genji's attitude. But Murasaki was more perceptive. He tried to restrain his feelings out of consideration for Murasaki, but in the end could not, and one moonlit evening after a rainfall, he lay down next to Tamakazura and confessed what was in his heart. She was surprised and perplexed, experiencing the first of many days of worry.

蛍（*Hotaru*）Fireflies

25 | 蛍 ほたる

　源氏の思いがけない愛の告白に、玉鬘たまかずらは困惑していました。一方で源氏は、異母弟にあたる蛍兵部卿ほたるひょうぶきょうの宮との交際をそそのかしたりします。玉鬘は源氏から逃れたいという気持ちもあって、以前よりは宮に心動いていました。

　五月雨さみだれの夜、蛍兵部卿の宮が玉鬘を訪れました。源氏は頃合ころあいを見計らって、玉鬘の近くに蛍を放ち、その光に浮かぶ美しい玉鬘の姿を見せました。宮は、源氏の思惑通り、ますます玉鬘への思いをつのらせるのでした。そして、源氏もまた玉鬘への慕情に苦悩していました。

　例年にない長雨をもてあまし、六条院の女君たちは物語で退屈を紛らわしていました。中でも田舎育ちの玉鬘は、珍しがって読んでいます。源氏は玉鬘を相手に、史実よりも物語のほうが真実を描いていることがあるなどと、物語論を語ります。また、紫の上むらさき うえとも、明石あかしの姫君に読ませる物語について話しあうのでした。

　一方、内大臣(もとの頭とうの中将)は、自分の姫君たちが思い通りにならないのを悲観し、評判の玉鬘を養育する源氏に刺激され、昔、行方不明になった夕顔ゆうがおとの間に出来た姫君(玉鬘)を見つけだしたいと、夢占いで判じさせるのでした。

Fireflies (*Hotaru*)

Genji's unexpected confession left Tamakazura at a loss. But at the same time, he pushed her to look favorably on the suit of his younger half-brother, Prince Hotaru, the Minister of War. Anxious to escape from Genji, she found Hotaru increasingly attractive.

One night during the summer rains, Hotaru visited her. At an opportune moment, Genji released fireflies, their light showing off Tamakazura's beauty. As Genji had calculated, his brother fell even deeper in love at the sight. But his own attraction to her remained a torment.

In the unusually long rains, time hung heavy on the Rokujō ladies, and they alleviated their boredom with romantic tales. Raised in the country, Tamakazura read them with avid curiosity, and at one point Genji engaged her in a discussion of literature in general, in which he argued that it was fiction, rather than history, that was the more true to life. He also talked with Murasaki about the works she was reading to her little ward, the Akashi Princess.

Palace Minister Tō no Chūjō, meanwhile, was dissatisfied that his plans for his own daughters were not proceeding as he wished. Spurred by Genji's adoption of the popular Tamakazura, he summoned a diviner to discover the whereabouts of his lost daughter by Yūgao, not realizing that it was Tamakazura herself.

常夏（*Tokonatsu*）Wild Pinks

26 常　夏

　暑い夏の日、源氏が夕霧と涼をとっていると、内大臣（もと
の頭の中将）の子息たちが訪ねてきました。源氏は、内大臣が
最近引き取ったという落胤の娘である近江の君のことを話題に
し、夕霧と雲居の雁の仲を割いたこともあって、内大臣を皮肉
るのでした。

　夕方、源氏はその公達（貴族の子息）たちを連れて、玉鬘のい
る西の対を訪ねました。玉鬘は源氏の口ぶりから、内大臣と不
仲らしいと察して悲しみます。源氏は玉鬘に和琴（日本固有の
六弦の琴）を教えながら、亡き母夕顔の昔話を語り、いずれ内
大臣と会わせることを約束するのでした。

　源氏は玉鬘の将来を思い、蛍兵部卿の宮か鬚黒の右大将と結
婚させようかと考えますが、自らの恋心はつのる一方で、なか
なか決心はつきません。

　一方、内大臣は、雲居の雁と夕霧の結婚も考えないではない
のですが、源氏のほうから折れてこないことに不満があったの
です。加えて、せっかく尋ねだした近江の君は品がなく、全く
姫君らしくない人柄に頭を悩ませていました。内大臣は、行儀
見習いを兼ねて、近江の君を弘徽殿の女御の女房として出仕さ
せることにしました。

Wild Pinks (*Tokonatsu*)

One day when Genji and his son Yūgiri were trying to avoid the summer heat, Palace Minister Tō no Chūjō's sons came to call. Genji asked after Lady Ōmi, whom Tō no Chūjō had brought into his home, and partly in view of the Minister's opposition to a match between their children Yūgiri and Kumoi no Kari, indulged in some sarcastic observations.

That evening, Genji took the young noblemen to Tamakazura's west wing. From the tone of Genji's remarks, she was distressed to realize that he and Tō no Chūjō had had a falling out. While instructing her in the art of the six-string *koto*, Genji spoke of her dead mother Yūgao and promised to let her meet her real father, the Palace Minister, one day.

Thinking of her best interests, Genji hoped to marry her either to Prince Hotaru or General Higekuro. But he found his own heart ever harder to govern and kept postponing the decision.

Palace Minister Tō no Chūjō, too, had his mind on a marriage, one between his daughter Kumoi no Kari and Genji's son Yūgiri. But he was piqued at Genji's failure to give in and come to him first. More galling was the discovery that Lady Ōmi, the long-lost daughter he had taken such trouble to find, was coarse and ill-bred. To improve her deportment, he decided to make her a lady-in-waiting to his daughter, Junior Consort Kokiden.

篝火 (*Kagaribi*) Fire Baskets

27 篝火

　近江の君を世間中が物笑いの種として噂しているのを耳にした源氏は、軽率な行動をした内大臣（もとの頭の中将）を批判します。玉鬘はそうした噂を聞くにつけても、実の娘でもない自分を引き取って、大切に扱ってくれている源氏に感謝し、次第に心を開いていくのでした。

　初秋の夕月夜、源氏は篝火を焚いて、琴を枕に玉鬘と添い臥します。それ以上の振る舞いはしないものの、源氏は切ない恋の思いを歌に託して玉鬘に訴えます。

　そこへ、夕霧のいる東の対から、内大臣の子息の柏木や弁の少将の楽の音が聞こえてきました。源氏は三人を西の対に招き、合奏するのでした。

　玉鬘が実の姉という真実を知らない柏木は、玉鬘を意識しながら緊張して和琴を弾くのでした。

Fire Baskets (*Kagaribi*)

Rumors reached Genji that Lady Ōmi was a laughingstock, and he criticized Tō no Chūjō's impulsive decision to bring her publicly into his house. Tamakazura heard the gossip too, and she began to appreciate the care Genji had given her despite the fact that they were not related, and she thought better of him.

One moonlit night in early autumn, Genji had fire baskets lit then lay down with Tamakazura, their heads resting on a *koto*. Though he made no actual overtures, he expressed his painful feelings of love in a poem to her.

Then came the sound of music from Yūgiri's apartments in the east wing, played by the young man and Tō no Chūjō's sons Kashiwagi and Ben no Shōshō. Genji invited the three young men to the west wing, where they all played music together. → bonding through art form/self expression

Kashiwagi, acutely attracted to Tamakazura, was all nerves as he played, unaware that she was actually his older half-sister.

野分 (*Nowaki*) The Typhoon

28 | 野分（のわき）

　六条院の秋好中宮（あきこのむちゅうぐう）のお庭では、秋の草花が美しく咲き乱れ、中宮をはじめとする人々の目を楽しませていました。

　八月、例年になく激しい野分（台風）が吹き荒れ、せっかくの花々も皆なぎ倒されてしまいました。その夕方、嵐の見舞いに春の御殿を訪れた夕霧（ゆうぎり）は、偶然紫の上（むらさきのうえ）を垣間見て、春の曙の霞の間に咲き乱れる樺桜のような気高い美しさに心を奪われます。

　翌朝、夕霧は花散里（はなちるさと）を見舞った後、源氏と紫の上を訪ねます。源氏は夕霧のどこか呆然としている様子に、紫の上を見られたかもしれないと思います。

　源氏が秋好中宮、明石（あかし）の君、玉鬘（たまかずら）、花散里を見舞うのにお供した夕霧は、源氏と玉鬘の親子らしからぬ振る舞いに驚くのでした。玉鬘の美しさは露を帯びた夕映えの八重山吹（やえやまぶき）のようでした。

　さらに明石の姫君を訪ねた夕霧は、姫君を垣間見て、風になびく藤の花のような美しさだと思いました。そして、逢えない雲居の雁（くもいのかり）を思い出し、硯（すずり）を借りて恋文をしたためるのでした。

The Typhoon (*Nowaki*)

The garden of Empress Akikonomu's quarter of the Rokujō Mansion was filled with gorgeous autumn blossoms, giving the lady and everyone else who chanced to see them great pleasure. But in the eighth month a typhoon of unusual force ruined them all. That evening, Yūgiri went round to the Spring Quarter to see how those within had weathered the storm, and by accident he caught a glimpse of Murasaki and was captivated by her regal beauty, quite like a cherry tree blossoming in profusion in the haze of a spring dawn.

The next morning he looked in on Hanachirusato, then called on Genji and Murasaki. Genji gathered from his son's flustered demeanor that he had seen his wife.

Yūgiri then accompanied his father on his rounds to Empress Akikonomu, the Akashi Lady, Hanachirusato, and Tamakazura and was surprised by Genji's distinctly unfatherly conduct toward the last of these. She shone like a dewy mountain rose in the evening sun.

And when the young man called on the Akashi Princess and happened to catch sight of her, he thought her beautiful as wisteria blossoms swaying in the wind. His thoughts turned to Kumoi no Kari, from whom he had been separated, and he borrowed an inkstone to write her a love note.

行幸（*Miyuki*）The Royal Outing

29 | 行幸

　源氏三十六歳の年の十二月、冷泉帝(源氏と藤壺の不義の子)
の大原野への行幸がありました。見物に出かけた玉鬘は、行列
の中に、はじめて実父の内大臣(もとの頭の中将)の姿を見つけ
ます。また、蛍兵部卿の宮や鬚黒の大将の姿も目にしますが、
源氏に似た、美しく端正な帝に目を奪われ、源氏から勧められ
ている宮仕えに気持ちが傾くのでした。

　翌年、源氏は玉鬘の入内を進めるために、裳着(女子の成人
式)の儀式を計画し、この機会に内大臣に玉鬘の真相を打ち明
けようと、裳の腰結い役(袴の腰紐を結ぶ役)を依頼します。と
ころが、内大臣は母大宮の病気を口実に断ってきました。

　源氏は亡き葵の上の母にあたる大宮を見舞った際、玉鬘の素
性を明かし、取りなしを頼みます。その場に内大臣が呼ばれ、
源氏の口から玉鬘が、探していた夕顔と自分の間に出来た姫君
だと聞かされ驚きます。内大臣は今まで隠していた源氏に疑念
を抱かずにはいられませんでしたが、育ててくれたことに感謝
し、腰結い役を引き受けることにしました。

　そして裳着の儀式の日、ようやく父娘の対面が果たされたの
でした。

The Royal Outing (*Miyuki*)

Genji was now thirty-six. In the last month of the year, Emperor Reizei, his illicit son by Fujitsubo, made an imperial progress to Ōharano. Tamakazura went out to view the procession and had her first glimpse of her real father, Tō no Chūjō, the Palace Minister. She also saw Prince Hotaru and General Higekuro, but her eye was particularly drawn to the Emperor, handsome and correct, who so resembled his father. She found herself inclining toward Genji's proposal that she enter Reizei's service.

As a first step to that end, Genji planned her coming-of-age festivities the following year, meaning to tell Tō no Chūjō the secret of his ward and offer him the honor of putting on her ceremonial train. But Tō no Chūjō excused himself on the grounds that his mother, Princess Ōmiya, was ill.

Genji then called on the ailing woman, the mother of his late wife Aoi, told her the secret of Tamakazura, and asked her to intercede with her son. She summoned Tō no Chūjō directly, and he was astounded to hear from Genji's own mouth that the girl was his own daughter by Yūgao and the very lady for whom he had been searching. The Palace Minister was suspicious of Genji's having hidden the girl until now, but he also appreciated the care Genji had taken with her upbringing, and he therefore accepted the honor of putting on her train.

And so it was on the day of the ceremony that Tamakazura finally met her father face to face.

藤袴（*Fujibakama*）Purple Trousers

30 | 藤袴

　玉鬘は、尚侍として入内したとしても、秋好中宮や弘徽殿の女御と帝寵争いになるかもしれないと懸念し、出仕をためらっていました。

　秋、祖母大宮の喪に服している玉鬘のところへ、源氏の使いとして帝の意向を伝えるため夕霧が訪ねてきました。夕霧は玉鬘が実の姉ではないと知り、恋心が芽生え、祖母大宮の服喪に寄せて、藤袴の花を御簾から差し入れて歌を詠み、自分の胸中を打ち明けます。しかし玉鬘はそんな夕霧をわずらわしく思います。冷たくあしらわれた夕霧は源氏のもとに戻り、世間で噂になっていることにかこつけ、玉鬘に対する源氏の本心を問いただすのでした。

　源氏は自分の潔白を示すべく、ついに玉鬘の出仕の日取りを決定します。それを知った鬚黒の大将は焦り、玉鬘の兄である柏木を通じて結婚を申し込んできました。冷泉帝の信望が厚い鬚黒との結婚に、鬚黒の将来性を見込んでいる玉鬘の実父の内大臣は心が動きます。

　玉鬘のもとには、鬚黒をはじめ求婚者たちから次々と恋文が届けられましたが、玉鬘は鬚黒を無視し、蛍兵部卿の宮（源氏の異母弟）にだけ返歌をするのでした。

Purple Trousers (*Fujibakama*)

Tamakazura hesitated to enter the service of the Emperor as a Principal Handmaid, knowing she might become embroiled in a bitter rivalry with Empress Akikonomu and Junior Consort Kokiden for his affections.

That autumn, Yūgiri went as Genji's messenger to convey the Emperor's goodwill to Tamakazura, who was then in mourning for her late grandmother, Princess Ōmiya. Now aware that she was not his real elder sister, Yūgiri had become attracted to her, and with their grandmother's death as a pretext, he pushed a bouquet of "purple trousers" beneath her blinds, at the same time reciting a poem that expressed his feelings for her. But Tamakazura thought his affections could only lead to trouble. Chastened by her coldness, Yūgiri returned to Genji, and under the pretext that rumors were now flying about his father's relationship with the woman, he asked to know the truth.

To demonstrate his innocence, Genji finally set the day for Tamakazura to go into court service. Moved to action by the news, General Higekuro proposed marriage to her via her elder brother Kashiwagi. Her father, Palace Minister Tō no Chūjō, smiled on the idea, knowing that the General had the ear of Emperor Reizei, and bright prospects.

But Tamakazura was receiving love letters from all manner of suitors beside the General, and she ignored him, choosing to answer only Genji's younger half-brother, Prince Hotaru.

Clothing used as a gift for courtship

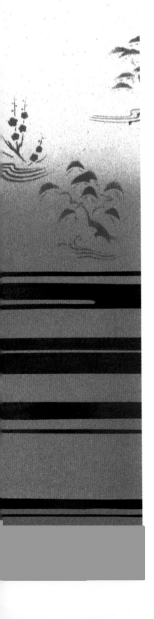

真木柱（*Makibashira*） The Cypress Pillar

31 真木柱

　玉鬘は、意外にも鬚黒の大将に嫁ぐことになりました。源氏は不本意ながらも、婿として丁重に遇します。冷泉帝も失望しますが、予定通り尚侍として出仕させることにしました。玉鬘もこの結婚には気が進まず、鬚黒だけが自邸に迎える準備にいそしんでいるのでした。

　鬚黒の北の方（正妻）は、ここ数年、物の怪に取り憑かれて病んでいましたが、ある雪の夜、玉鬘のもとに出かけようとする鬚黒に、突然北の方が、鬚黒の背後から香炉の灰を浴びせかけるという事件が起きました。

　それ以来、鬚黒は北の方（紫の上の異母姉妹）のもとに寄りつかなくなり、激怒した北の方の父の式部卿の宮（もとの兵部卿の宮）は、北の方と子供らを実家に引き取ることにしました。真木柱の姫君は父の鬚黒と離れるのがいやで、自邸を去り難く、

> 今はとて宿離れぬとも馴れきつる
> 　　真木の柱はわれを忘るな
>
> 〈今を限りと、私が育ったこの家を離れてしまっても、馴れ親しんだ真木の柱は私を忘れないで。〉

という悲嘆の歌を詠み、柱の割れ目に紙を押し入れて、泣く泣く母とともに牛車に乗り込むのでした。

　鬚黒は式部卿の宮邸へ赴きますが、北の方はもちろん、式部卿の宮にも病気を理由に面会を断られ、何とか二人の若君だけを連れ戻すことができただけでした。

　翌年春、予定通り玉鬘は出仕しました。しかしすぐ鬚黒は強引に、自邸に退出させてしまいます。

　十一月、玉鬘は男子を出産しました。

The Cypress Pillar (*Makibashira*)

In the end, Tamakazura defied expectations and married General Higekuro. Though not his first choice, Genji treated him as a son-in-law. Emperor Reizei was disappointed, too, but honored his offer to her of service at court. The lady herself was lukewarm about the marriage, and Higekuro alone busily set about preparing his mansion to welcome his new bride.

Higekuro's principal wife had been deranged for the last several years, the victim of spirit possession. One snowy night as Higekuro was preparing to visit Tamakazura, she came up from behind and poured ashes from a censer over him.

Higekuro ceased thereafter to visit his first wife (Lady Murasaki's half-sister), and her angry father, Prince Shikibu, the Minister of Rites (formerly known as Prince Hyōbu, the Minister of War), took her back into his house with her children. Princess Makibashira (Cypress Pillar) hated to leave her father Higekuro and her old home, and she wrote a mournful poem before setting out:

> The time has come
> for me to leave this house—
> O cypress pillar
> that I have learned to love,
> please do not forget me!

She poked the poem into a crack in a pillar and, weeping, stepped into the ox carriage with her mother.

Higekuro called at the mansion of Prince Shikibu but his wife refused to see him, as did the Prince himself, protesting illness. All Higekuro was able to do was bring back his two sons.

Next spring, Tamakazura went into court service as planned. But soon thereafter Higekuro made her return to his home.

In the eleventh month, she gave birth to a son.

梅枝（*Umegae*） A Branch of Plum

32 | 梅枝
（うめ　がえ）

　娘の明石の姫君の東宮（後の今上帝）入内が近づき、源氏は、裳着の儀式（女子の成人式）の準備に余念がありません。正月末、公私ともに暇な頃でしたので、源氏は薫物合わせを思い立ち、六条院の女君と朝顔の前斎院に香の調合を依頼します。

　二月十日、蛍兵部卿の宮を判者として、薫物合わせが行われました。朝顔の前斎院からは、梅の花とともに「黒方」が届けられ、ほかの女君からも趣向を凝らした香が次々と届けられました。蛍兵部卿の宮は、どれをとっても素晴らしい香を、それぞれに誉めたたえたのでした。その夜は源氏、蛍兵部卿の宮、柏木、夕霧の管絃に、弁の少将が「梅が枝」を謡う風流な宴が行われました。

　翌日、明石の姫君の裳着の儀式が行われ、秋好中宮が腰結い役をつとめました。

　二十日過ぎ、東宮が元服し、明石の姫君の入内は四月と決まりました。源氏は姫君に持たせる調度に、書道の手本を加えることにし、自らも筆をとります。また、蛍兵部卿の宮や紫の上と名筆について論じるのでした。

　内大臣（もとの頭の中将）は、明石の姫君入内のことを耳にするにつけても、わが娘の雲居の雁の身の振り方に頭を悩ませていました。源氏も夕霧に対して、結婚したほうがいいと訓戒するのでした。雲居の雁は夕霧の縁談の噂を聞き、夕霧に恨みの歌を送りますが、夕霧の、雲居の雁を思う気持ちに変わりはないのでした。

A Branch of Plum (*Umegae*)

The date approached for the Akashi Princess to enter the service of the Crown Prince (the future Emperor), and Genji devoted himself to preparations for her coming-of-age ceremony. Freed at the end of the first month from pressing public and private obligations, Genji hit upon the idea to have an incense competition, and he asked the former Kamo Priestess Asagao and the Rokujō ladies to prepare the necessary fragrances.

The contest was held on the tenth of the second month, with Prince Hotaru as judge. A scent called "Kurobō" came from the former Priestess together with some plum blossoms, and carefully prepared entries arrived in turn from the other ladies as well. Each one was the equal of the next, and Prince Hotaru lavishly praised them all. That evening Ben no Shōshō sang "A Branch of Plum" at an elegant soirée, accompanied by the pipes and strings of the Prince, Genji, Kashiwagi, and Yūgiri.

The Princess's coming-of-age ceremony was held the following day, with Empress Akikonomu having the honor of putting on the ceremonial train.

After the twentieth, the Crown Prince was likewise initiated into adulthood, and it was arranged that the Akashi Princess would enter his service in the fourth month. As part of her trousseau, Genji included a collection of models for calligraphy practice, with some of his own work included, and he talked about calligraphy with Prince Hotaru, Murasaki, and others.

The news of the Akashi Princess's entrance into court service reached Palace Minister Tō no Chūjō, causing him worry about the future of his own daughter, Kumoi no Kari. At the same time, Genji lectured his son Yūgiri on the desirability of marriage. Hearing rumors that Yūgiri was to be betrothed, Kumoi no Kari sent him an angry poem, but his feelings for her remained strong as ever.

藤裏葉 (*Fuji no uraba*) Wisteria Leaves

33 藤裏葉

　父である内大臣(もとの頭の中将)に仲を割かれたままの雲居の雁と、夕霧(源氏と葵の上の子)との相思相愛の仲に変わりはありませんでした。内大臣は夕霧の縁談の噂を聞いて焦っていました。

　大宮の三回忌の際、ついに内大臣は態度を軟化させ、自分のほうから夕霧に話しかけます。

　四月、自邸の藤の花の宴に夕霧を招き、ついに二人の結婚を許し、夕霧と雲居の雁は長年の恋を実らせ、ようやく結ばれたのでした。

　四月二十日過ぎ、明石の姫君入内に際し、紫の上が付き添いますが、後見役は生母の明石の君に譲ることにしました。後見の交替の折、二人ははじめて対面し、互いのすぐれた人柄を認め合うのでした。明石の君と姫君の母娘も、大堰で雪の日に別れて以来、ようやく再会を果たしたのでした。源氏は、今はもう万事安心と、出家の志を深くするのでした。

　来年、四十歳を迎える源氏は、冷泉帝より准太上天皇の位を授けられ、内大臣は太政大臣、夕霧は中納言にそれぞれ昇進しました。夕霧と雲居の雁は、共に幼い頃を過ごした、思い出の家である亡き祖母大宮の三条邸に住むことになりました。

　十月、冷泉帝の六条院への行幸に、朱雀院も加わるという異例の華々しい盛儀がありました。

　この年、源氏の栄華は絶頂を迎えていました。

Wisteria Leaves (*Fuji no Uraba*)

Although Palace Minister Tō no Chūjō had separated his daughter Kumoi no Kari from Genji's son Yūgiri, the two young people were still in love. And the Minister himself was stung by rumors that Yūgiri was to be wed to someone else.

On the occasion of the third anniversary of the death of his mother, Princess Ōmiya, he finally abandoned his opposition to the match and took it upon himself to bring up the matter with Yūgiri.

In the fourth month, he invited the young man to a wisteria-viewing party at his mansion and finally consented to the marriage. The couple's long devotion was at last rewarded.

After the twentieth of the fourth month, the Akashi Princess went into court service. Murasaki accompanied her for the event but relinquished her guardianship to the Princess's mother, the Akashi Lady. It was on this occasion that the two older women met for the first time, and each recognized the fine qualities of the other. It was also the first time mother and daughter had met since parting on that snowy day in Ōi long ago. Satisfied that all was now in order, Genji began to think about taking holy vows.

He turned forty the next year and was awarded by Reizei a rank equivalent to that of a retired emperor. Palace Minister Tō no Chūjō became Chancellor, and Yūgiri was promoted to Middle Counselor. Together with his bride Kumoi no Kari, Yūgiri moved into the memory-filled Sanjō Mansion of their late grandmother Princess Ōmiya where they had both spent their childhoods.

In the tenth month, Reizei made an imperial progress to the Rokujō Mansion, an event made all the more splendid by the unprecedented participation of Retired Emperor Suzaku.

It was that year when Genji reached the height of his glory.

若菜 (*Wakana*) Young Greens

34 若菜

〈上〉

　朱雀院(源氏の異母兄)は、重い病のため出家を考えていましたが、最愛の娘女三の宮の処遇に苦慮していました。院は悩んだ末、源氏に嫁がせることにします。源氏ははじめこそ辞退したものの、女三の宮が亡き藤壺の中宮の姪にあたることを思い出し、承諾するのでした。

　源氏四十歳の二月、女三の宮が正妻として六条院に降嫁してきました。紫の上は平静を装っていたものの、その動揺は大きいものでした。一方、源氏は女三の宮の幼さに失望しました。

　翌年三月末、六条院で蹴鞠が催され、夕霧と柏木は、偶然、猫によって引き上げられた御簾の内にいた女三の宮を見てしまいます。以前から女三の宮を慕っていた柏木は思いが通じたのかと、恋情を燃え上がらせるのでした。

〈下〉

　柏木は、女三の宮の猫を手に入れ、宮への思いをこめて愛玩します。

　四年後、冷泉帝が譲位し、明石の女御の皇子が東宮となりました。朱雀院五十の賀宴を計画した源氏は、女三の宮に琴の伝授を日夜行い、賀宴に先立ち、六条院の女君たちを集めて女楽を催します。翌日夜、紫の上が突然発病し二条院に移されました。

　一方、柏木は女三の宮の姉である女二の宮(落葉の宮)と結婚したものの、やはり女三の宮への思いは断ち切れず、源氏が看病のために六条院を留守にしていたある日、女三の宮のもとに忍び入り、ついに契ってしまいます。

　その後、女三の宮が懐妊し、不審に思っていた源氏は、柏木からの文を発見して密通を知ります。六条院での賀宴の試楽の折、柏木は源氏から痛烈な皮肉と眼ざしを浴びせられ、病床に臥す身となるのでした。

Young Greens (*Wakana*)

PART ONE

Retired Emperor Suzaku (Genji's elder half-brother) was seriously ill, but concerns for the welfare of his favorite child, the Third Princess, prevented him from taking holy orders. After much worry, he decided to marry her to Genji. Genji at first refused, but he finally agreed in view of her being the niece of the late Empress Fujitsubo.

In the second month of Genji's fortieth year, the Third Princess came to live at Rokujō Mansion as his principal wife. Murasaki accepted the news with outward calm and inner turmoil. Genji, for his part, was disappointed by the Third Princess's immaturity.

The next year at the end of the third month, a kickball match was held at Rokujō, and at one point Yūgiri and Kashiwagi caught sight of the Third Princess when her cat became tangled in one of the blinds and exposed her to view. She had long been on Kashiwagi's mind, and now, thinking his devotion had been rewarded, he fell hopelessly in love.

PART TWO

Kashiwagi acquired the Third Princess's cat and cherished it as a memento.

Four years later, Emperor Reizei abdicated, and the son of the Akashi Junior Consort was made Crown Prince. Genji was planning a celebration in honor of Retired Emperor Suzaku's fiftieth birthday and, in preparation, was intensively training the Third Princess in the art of the *koto*. As a rehearsal for the main event, he assembled his Rokujō ladies and had them perform a concert. The following night Murasaki suddenly fell ill and was moved to the Nijō Mansion.

Kashiwagi, meanwhile, had been married to the Third Princess's elder sister, Princess Ochiba (Fallen Leaves), but he could not stop longing for the Third Princess herself. One day when Genji was away from Rokujō nursing Murasaki, Kashiwagi stole in on the Third Princess and slept with her.

She became pregnant, and Genji's suspicions were confirmed when he discovered a letter to her from Kashiwagi. During a rehearsal at the Rokujō Mansion for Retired Emperor Suzaku's birthday celebration, Kashiwagi felt the bitter edge of Genji's sarcastic remarks and reproachful looks, and he fell seriously ill thereafter.

柏木（*Kashiwagi*）The Oak Tree

35 | 柏木

　正月、柏木の病状は悪化するばかりでした。死が近いことを悟った柏木は、女三の宮に胸の内を訴える手紙を送ります。短い返事を書いた女三の宮は、その夕方から産気づき、翌朝、不義の子（薫）を出産しました。

　出産後、女三の宮は産後の衰弱に加え、源氏の冷たい態度におびえて、源氏に出家を願い出たのですが、制止されます。そんな娘を心配し、夜半ひそかに見舞いに訪れた父の朱雀院に懇願して、女三の宮は出家してしまいます。実は、女三の宮をこのようにしむけたのは、故六条の御息所の死霊が取り憑いたしわざでした。

　女三の宮の出家を聞いて危篤状態に陥った柏木は、見舞いに来た親友の夕霧に真相をほのめかし、源氏への詫びと、妻の女二の宮（落葉の宮）のことを託し、まもなく他界しました。

　三月、若君（薫）の誕生から五十日目の祝儀が盛大に行われました。ただ尼姿の女三の宮を前にして、心なしか柏木に似ている若君を抱いた源氏は、複雑な気持ちになるのでした。

　夕霧は、柏木の遺言通り、未亡人になった落葉の宮を見舞うのですが、同情が次第に恋情へと変わってゆくのでした。

The Oak Tree (*Kashiwagi*)

The new year came, and Kashiwagi's illness only worsened. Realizing he was near death, he wrote the Third Princess a letter baring his soul to her. She wrote a brief reply and, that very evening, was seized by labor pains. She gave birth to their illicit son, Kaoru, the next morning.

Weak from the birth and fearful of Genji's coldness, she told him she wished to take holy orders, but he forbade her. After receiving the entreaties of Retired Emperor Suzaku, however, who called on him late one night in secret out of concern for his daughter, Genji acquiesced to her request. The Third Princess's condition was again the work of the tormented spirit of the late Rokujō.

When Kashiwagi heard that the Third Princess had taken vows, his illness reached the final stage, and he hinted at the reason when his friend Yūgiri came to look in on him. After asking Yūgiri to apologize to Genji and look after his wife, Princess Ochiba, he passed away.

In the third month, a grand ceremony was held to mark the fiftieth day after the birth. But Genji's feelings were decidedly mixed in the presence of the Third Princess in her nun's habit and the baby who so painfully resembled the dead Kashiwagi.

Yūgiri respected Kashiwagi's last request to look after his widow, and his sympathy gradually turned to love.

横笛（*Yokobue*）The Flute

36 横笛

　柏木の一周忌をむかえ、源氏の特別手厚い供養に、柏木の父致仕の大臣（引退した大臣、もとの頭の中将）は感激します。夕霧も未亡人、落葉の宮への見舞いを続けていました。

　朱雀院から、女三の宮に送られてきた筍をかじる無邪気な薫の姿を見た源氏は、何の罪もないこの子を捨てるわけにはいかないと思うのでした。

　夕霧は、柏木の遺言に不審を抱いていましたが、真相を源氏に聞きかねていました。

　秋、夕霧は落葉の宮のいる一条の宮邸を訪れました。子どもが多く騒がしいわが邸に比べ、一条の宮邸のひっそりと落ち着いたたたずまいに、夕霧は心休まるのでした。宮の母の御息所と故人の思い出を語った後、夕霧が琵琶をとって「想夫恋」を弾くと、御簾の奥で落葉の宮も琴を弾き合奏するのでした。その帰り際、夕霧は御息所から形見として柏木遺愛の横笛を贈られました。

　夕霧の妻の雲居の雁は、夕霧が最近、落葉の宮のところに通っているという噂を聞いて、不機嫌でした。帰邸した夕霧は、その夜の夢に柏木の亡霊を見ます。夢の柏木は、笛を伝えたい人は別にいると告げるのでした。

　源氏に夢の報告をし、笛の処置を相談しようと、六条院を訪れた夕霧は、明石の女御の皇子たちと遊んでいる薫を見て、心なしか柏木に似ていると感じます。夕霧から夢の話と柏木の遺言を聞かされた源氏は、笛だけ預かり、遺言には言葉を濁すのでした。

The Flute (*Yokobue*)

On the first anniversary of Kashiwagi's death, Genji held particularly fine services, and Kashiwagi's father, the Retired Chancellor Tō no Chūjō, was deeply moved. Yūgiri, meanwhile, continued to pay visits of condolence to Princess Ochiba.

Watching little Kaoru munch guilelessly on bamboo shoots sent to the Third Princess by Retired Emperor Suzaku, Genji realized that he could never abandon the innocent child.

Yūgiri continued to have suspicions about the truth behind Kashiwagi's last wishes, but he found it impossible to broach the subject with his father.

That autumn, Yūgiri paid another call on Princess Ochiba in the Ichijō Mansion, and he found its quiet atmosphere a relaxing change from his own home, teeming with the clamor of numerous children. After chatting with the Princess's mother, Miyasudokoro, about Kashiwagi, Yūgiri took up a lute and played "I Long for Him," whereupon the Princess began to accompany him from behind the blinds on her *koto*. When he left, the mother gave him her dead son's prized flute as a keepsake.

Yūgiri's wife, Kumoi no Kari, was put out at rumors that her husband had recently been visiting Princess Ochiba. When he returned that night, he dreamt that Kashiwagi came to him and announced that he had wanted the flute to go to someone else.

Yūgiri went to the Rokujō Mansion to tell Genji of the dream and ask him what to do with the flute. Watching little Kaoru playing with the children of the Akashi Junior Consort, he was painfully aware of how much he resembled Kashiwagi. And when Genji heard of the dream and of Kashiwagi's last request, Genji relieved Yūgiri of the flute but was otherwise evasive.

鈴虫（*Suzumushi*）Bell Crickets

37 鈴虫

　蓮の花が盛りの夏のころ、尼となった女三の宮の持仏開眼供養が営まれました。源氏は仏具一式を用意し、紫の上も準備を手伝います。御帳台をかりの仏壇にした部屋で、若い尼姿の宮を前に、今更ながら源氏は、宮を出家させてしまったことを悔やむのでした。宮は、父朱雀院から源氏との別居を勧められますが、源氏は六条院から手放そうとはしませんでした。

　秋、源氏は女三の宮の住む御殿の庭を、秋の野らしく造り直して虫を放し、風の涼しくなった夕暮れに訪れ、女三の宮に未練を訴えます。女三の宮はそんな源氏をうとましく思い、住まいを移りたいと思うのでした。

　中秋の名月の夜、源氏は女三の宮の御殿を訪れ、庭に放した鈴虫の声を聞きながら、宮と歌を交わし、琴を弾いていました。そこへ蛍兵部卿の宮や夕霧たちが訪れてきて管絃の宴がはじまりました。続いて冷泉院から月見の宴の招きがあり、一同は参上し、詩歌を作ったり、音楽を愉しみます。

　翌朝、源氏は秋好中宮を訪ねました。中宮は亡き母の六条の御息所の怨霊が、紫の上や女三の宮に取り憑いたという噂を聞いて、その妄執を晴らすために出家したいと打ち明けます。源氏は出家に反対し、追善供養を勧めるのでした。

Bell Crickets (*Suzumushi*)

In the summer when the lotus blossoms were at their height, a ceremony was held to dedicate a tutelary statue for the chapel of the Cloistered Third Princess. Genji prepared the holy accouterments, and Murasaki, too, helped with the preparations. There with the young Third Princess in her nun's habit, before the sleeping dais doubling as a sanctuary, Genji was struck with belated sadness that he had let her take religious vows. For her part, she had asked her father, the Retired Emperor Suzaku, to recommend to Genji that they live apart, but Genji refused to let her leave his Rokujō Mansion.

That autumn, Genji had bell crickets released into the garden of the quarter where she was living, which he had had done over as an autumnal moor, and called on her in the cool evening breeze. He spoke of his lingering tender thoughts, which offended her and made her wish she could live elsewhere.

He visited again on the night of the full autumn moon, and while listening to the crickets in the garden, he exchanged poems with the Third Princess and played *koto* music. A number of others then came to call, including Prince Hotaru and Yūgiri, and they made a concert of it. Then they received a moon-viewing invitation from Retired Emperor Reizei, and the men left for the palace, where they enjoyed more music, and poetry in Japanese and Chinese.

The next morning, Genji called on Empress Akikonomu. She told him that she had heard rumors that the spirit of her dead mother, Rokujō, had possessed both Murasaki and the Third Princess, and she revealed that she wished to take holy vows herself to help dissipate the obsessions that bound her mother's spirit to the world. Genji opposed the notion and recommended prayer instead.

夕霧 (*Yūgiri*) Evening Mist

38 | 夕霧

夕霧は日ましに柏木の未亡人、落葉の宮に惹かれていました。落葉の宮は、母の一条の御息所の病気祈禱のため、洛北の小野に移りました。夕霧は小野まで訪ね、落葉の宮に恋心を訴えます。しかし、落葉の宮は夕霧を避けるばかりで、夕霧も無理にそれ以上の行為に出ず、深い霧を口実に宮の傍で過ごすものの、むなしく一夜を明かし、朝方帰っていったのでした。

夕霧のその朝帰りを見たという律師(祈禱をする僧)の話から、一条の御息所は二人の関係を誤解し、夕霧に、落葉の宮と本気で結婚する気かどうか確かめるために手紙を送ります。

ところがその手紙を、朝帰りに嫉妬した妻雲居の雁に奪い取られてしまいます。新婚二日目の夜と誤解している御息所は手紙の返事も来ず、夕霧も訪れて来ないことに落胆し、心労のあまり急逝してしまいました。

夕霧は葬儀一切を取りしきり、出家を願う落葉の宮を強引に一条の宮に連れ戻し、結婚を迫ります。落葉の宮は、母が死んだのは夕霧のせいもあると思っていたので、夕霧がいっそううとましく、塗籠(周囲を壁でぬりこめた閉鎖的な部屋。納戸)に閉じこもって抵抗しましたが、拒みきれず、ついに二人は一夜を共にします。

落葉の宮との結婚に立腹した夕霧の正妻の雲居の雁は、子どもを連れて実家である致仕の大臣のもとへ帰ってしまいました。夕霧はあわてて妻の実家にかけつけますが、雲居の雁は戻ろうとしません。夕霧には、雲居の雁や藤典侍との間に、すでにそれぞれたくさんの子どもがいるのでした。

Evening Mist (*Yūgiri*)

Daily, Yūgiri became more taken with Kashiwagi's widow, Princess Ochiba. Then the lady went from the Ichijō Mansion to Ono, north of the city, with her mother, Miyasudokoro, to have prayers said for her mother's illness. Yūgiri made the trip to visit her there, as well, where he confessed his love. But she only evaded him, and Yūgiri made no further attempts to persuade her. Using the mists as a pretext for not leaving, he spent the night by the Princess's side but returned to the capital the next morning without having made her his.

But the monk who was praying for Miyasudokoro told her that he saw Yūgiri leaving that morning, misleading her into sending Yūgiri a letter asking him whether or not he truly intended to marry her daughter.

The letter, however, was snatched away by Yūgiri's wife, Kumoi no Kari, who was jealous because he had stayed away all night. Miyasudokoro, mistakenly believing it was the second night of her daughter's marriage, was devastated when no reply to her letter came, much less a visit from Yūgiri himself, and her illness carried her off in consequence.

Yūgiri took charge of every aspect of the funeral and forced Princess Ochiba, intent on becoming a nun, to return to the Ichijō Mansion, where he redoubled his efforts to marry her. But she blamed him in part for her mother's death, and became even more obdurate. She locked herself in a strong room, but her resistance came to naught, and he finally slept with her.

Angry at the news of the marriage, Kumoi no Kari took the children and returned to the home of her father, the Retired Chancellor Tō no Chūjō. Frantic, Yūgiri hurried after her, but she refused to come back. Yūgiri had numerous children, both by Kumoi no Kari and by Koremitsu's daughter, Tō no Naishinosuke.

御法（*Minori*）The Holy Writ

39 御法<ruby>御<rt>み</rt></ruby><ruby>法<rt>のり</rt></ruby>

　<ruby>紫<rt>むらさき</rt></ruby>の<ruby>上<rt>うえ</rt></ruby>は、四年前の大病以来病がちになり、出家を強く望んでいました。しかし源氏は、自らも出家を志していながら、紫の上の出家を絶対に許そうとしません。

　三月、紫の上<ruby>発願<rt>ほつがん</rt></ruby>(願をかけること)の法華経千部供養が行われ、<ruby>帝<rt>みかど</rt></ruby>や東宮、<ruby>秋好<rt>あきこのむ</rt></ruby>中宮らをはじめとした人々がこぞって参列しました。紫の上は長くない命を感じ、<ruby>花散里<rt>はなちるさと</rt></ruby>や<ruby>明石<rt>あかし</rt></ruby>の君に別れの思いをこめて歌を交わすのでした。

　夏、紫の上はますます衰弱し、見舞いに来た明石の中宮に遺言めいたことを伝え、特に可愛がっている中宮の子の三の宮(<ruby>匂宮<rt>におうのみや</rt></ruby>)に、庭の紅梅と桜を形見として大切にし、仏に供えて欲しいとさりげなく遺言をするのでした。

　秋の夕暮れ、紫の上は源氏や明石の中宮と、はかない命を、庭に咲く萩に置かれた露にたとえて歌を詠み交わしました。その直後、紫の上の容態は急変し、中宮に手をとられたまま、夜明け頃静かに息を引き取ります。

　最愛の妻を失った源氏は茫然自失しますが、仏のご利益をいただくため、形ばかりでもと、<ruby>夕霧<rt>ゆうぎり</rt></ruby>に髪をおろす手配をさせます。葬送を終え、帝や<ruby>致仕<rt>ちじ</rt></ruby>の大臣(もとの頭の中将)らから、あいついで弔問がありますが、悲嘆にくれた源氏は出家しようと考えるばかりで、それも決心がつかないままひたすら仏道に専念するのでした。

The Holy Writ (*Minori*)

Murasaki had never completely recovered from her grave illness four years earlier, and she fervently desired to take holy vows. But Genji, while hoping to take vows himself, obdurately refused to let her do so.

In the third month, she consecrated a thousand copies of the *Lotus Sutra* that she had commissioned, and the Emperor, the Crown Prince, Empress Akikonomu, and everyone else of importance attended the ceremony. She sensed that she had little time left and wrote poems to Hanachirusato and the Akashi Lady that hinted at parting.

She grew weaker all summer, and when the Akashi Empress came to pay a sick call, Murasaki told the Empress her last requests. She also casually asked the Empress's little son, the Third Prince (Prince Niou), to care for the plum and cherry trees in the garden as keepsakes and to offer blossoms up from time to time to the Buddhas.

One evening in autumn, she exchanged poems with Genji and the Akashi Empress comparing the evanescence of life to dew on bush clover. She was then suddenly taken for the worse, and near dawn, holding the Empress's hand, she quietly breathed her last.

Genji was numb with grief at the loss of his favorite, but he was still able to ask Yūgiri to make arrangements so that she might have symbolic vows administered to accrue Buddhist merit in her next life. After the funeral, messages of condolence arrived from the Emperor, Retired Chancellor Tō no Chūjō, and many others. Genji in his grief resolved to quit the world for the monastery, but while he gave himself over to prayer, he could not bring himself to take the final steps and become a monk.

幻 (*Maboroshi*) The Wizard

幻

まぼろし

　年が明けても、源氏は紫の上（むらさき うえ）を失った悲しみに暮れるばかりでした。弟の蛍兵部卿の宮（ほたるひょうぶ きょう）以外には、年賀の挨拶に訪れてきた人と会おうともせず、昔から仕えている女房たちと思い出話をして紫の上を偲ぶ毎日を過ごしていました。

　春、紫の上の形見の紅梅を世話したり、桜の花が散らないように気づかう匂宮（におうのみや）の姿に、源氏の心はわずかながら慰められますが、女三の宮や明石（あかし）の君を訪れますと、いっそう紫の上が思い出されるのでした。

　四月、花散里（はなちるさと）から衣替えの装束が届けられました。ほととぎすの声、蓮の花、ひぐらしの声、撫子の花、蛍の光、七夕、何につけても故人が思い出されて、悲しみは癒えません。

　八月、一周忌を迎え、紫の上作製の曼陀羅や経を供養しました。九月に重陽（ちょうよう）の菊、十月に雁を見るにつけても、悲しみを新たにするのでした。

　年の暮れ、源氏は涙ながらに紫の上とやりとりした手紙などを焼いて身辺整理をし、出家の準備をはじめるのでした。御仏名会（おぶつ みょうえ）の日、源氏は紫の上の死後、はじめて人前に姿を現し、人々の涙をさそいます。

　十二月晦日、匂宮が鬼やらいの儀式にはしゃぐ姿を見て、源氏はもうこの可愛い姿を見ることもなくなるのだと思い、

もの思ふと過ぐる月日も知らぬ間に

年もわが世も今日や尽きぬる

〈物思いのために、過ぎる歳月にも気づかぬうちに、今年も、この私の人生も、今日で終わってしまうのだろうか。〉

と最後の歌を詠むのでした。

　源氏は、この帖を最後に物語から姿を消します。

The Wizard (*Maboroshi*)

The new year arrived, but Genji's sadness at the loss of Murasaki only deepened. Of those who came to proffer season's greetings, he was at home to none save his younger brother Hotaru, preferring to spend his days instead sharing memories of his dead wife with his senior ladies-in-waiting.

Prince Niou took good care of the trees Murasaki had left him in her memory, tending the plum and trying to keep the cherry blossoms from scattering. The sight provided Genji some small consolation, but his visits to the Third Princess and the Akashi Lady only reminded him of Murasaki all the more. *robes = new beginning → change of self, personality*

In the fourth month, clothes for the new season arrived from Hana-chirusato. Everything reminded him of the dead lady—the cuckoo's cry, the lotus blossoms, the evening cicadas, the pinks, the twinkling fireflies, the Festival of the Weaver Maid—and his gloom refused to dissipate.

The first anniversary of her death came in the eighth month, and Genji offered up a mandala and the sutras she had commissioned. His grief was only compounded by the Chrysanthemum Festival in the ninth month and the geese in the tenth.

At the end of the year Genji put his affairs in order in preparation for taking holy vows and wept as he consigned Murasaki's letters to the flames. His first public appearance since her death took place at the invocation of the holy names, and it brought tears to people's eyes.

On the last day of the year, watching Prince Niou scampering about exorcizing demons, Genji was struck by the thought that he had little time left to see that precious child, and he composed this final poem:

> Lost in sad thoughts,
> I did not notice
> the passing of the days and months;
> are this year and this life
> to draw to a close today?

(With this chapter, Genji disappears from the tale.)

雲隠 (*Kumogakure*) Hidden in the Clouds

41 | 雲 隠
くも　がくれ

　帖名だけで本文のない帖。

「雲隠」という言葉は光源氏の死を暗示しています。

「宿木」の帖によると、源氏は出家後、嵯峨に隠棲し、二、三
年後に死去したとあります。

Hidden in the Clouds (*Kumogakure*)

Only the chapter title, which implies the death of Genji, the Shining Prince, remains.

In the "Mistletoe" chapter that follows, it is related that Genji died two or three years after taking Buddhist vows and retiring to Saga.

匂宮（*Niou no miya*）The Perfumed Prince

42 匂宮

　光源氏が亡くなってからというもの、その声望を継ぐような
人物はなかなかいませんでしたが、今上帝と明石の中宮の間の
皇子の三の宮と、女三の宮の若君（柏木との不義の子）が美貌だ
と、評判になっていました。

　女三の宮の若君は、生まれながらに不思議な芳香を身に具え
ており、〈薫〉中将と呼ばれ、その薫と何かにつけて張り合って
いた三の宮は、薫に負けじと香をたきしめるうち、〈匂宮〉と呼
ばれるようになりました。人々はこの二人を並べてもてはやし
ていました。

　匂宮は紫の上から伝領した二条院に住み、祖父の光源氏から
情熱的で色好みの性格を受け継いでいます。それに対し、薫は、
自分の出生に何となく疑念を抱いて、物思いに沈みがちな若者
になっていました。

　夕霧（源氏と葵の上の子）は、雲居の雁と落葉の宮のもとに月
に十五日ずつ通っています。

　匂宮は冷泉帝の女一の宮に思いをつのらせていました。長女
を東宮に入内させている夕霧は、娘のうち一人は、匂宮か薫の
どちらかと結婚させたいと望みますが、匂宮にはその気があり
ません。

　正月、賭弓の競射が行われ、勝った組の大将夕霧は、饗宴を
六条院に用意し、匂宮や薫を招きました。

The Perfumed Prince (*Niou no Miya*)

Genji, the Shining Prince, was dead, and no one could take his place. But his grandson, the Third Prince, son of the present Emperor and the Akashi Empress, and his putative son by the Third Princess (actually the son of Kashiwagi) were particularly known for their good looks.

The Third Princess's son was known as Kaoru Chūjō, the Fragrant Captain, because of a marvellous natural scent that had been with him since birth. The Third Prince, in all things Kaoru's rival, compounded all sorts of incense to match Kaoru's, becoming known in consequence as Niou no Miya, the Perfumed Prince. Both young men were endlessly talked about and compared.

Niou, who lived in the Nijō Mansion that he had inherited from Murasaki, had Genji's passionate and sensual nature. Kaoru, by contrast, was more introspective, having vague doubts about the true circumstances of his birth.

Yūgiri, Genji's son by the late Aoi, was now married to Kumoi no Kari and Princess Ochiba, and he spent half a month with each.

He had sent his eldest daughter into the service of the Crown Prince, and he now hoped to marry another daughter to either Niou or Kaoru, but Niou was not interested. The young man instead took a growing interest in Emperor Reizei's daughter, the First Princess.

An archery contest in the first month was won by Yūgiri's team, and he held a banquet at Rokujō, to which he invited both young men.

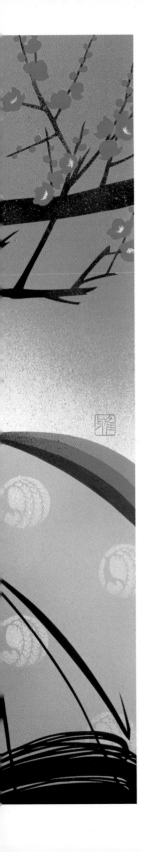

紅梅（*Kōbai*）The Rose Plum

43 紅梅 <ruby>紅<rt>こう</rt></ruby><ruby>梅<rt>ばい</rt></ruby>

　按察使の大納言（柏木の弟）の北の方が、一の姫君と中の姫君を遺して亡くなりました。大納言は後妻に、鬚黒の大臣の娘で、故蛍兵部卿の宮の未亡人となっていた真木柱を迎え、その間に男子をもうけました。

　真木柱は亡き夫との子、宮の姫君を連れ子としていました。大納言は、宮の姫君を実子と同じように扱おうとする一方で、好色な関心も寄せるのですが、大納言が部屋を訪ねても姿を見せず、琵琶の音色も聞かせてくれないという、どこかよそよそしい態度に腹を立てるのでした。また、姫君の優雅さも実の娘より優れているかも知れないと、内心不安に思うのでした。

　大納言は、一の姫君を東宮妃として入内させました。中の姫君の婿には匂宮を考えており、庭の、芳香を放つ紅梅の枝に歌を添えて、息子の大夫の君に持たせ、匂宮に贈って気を引こうとします。しかし、匂宮は、宮の姫君のほうに関心があるため、気乗りがしません。

　匂宮は、大夫の君に文使いをさせて、宮の姫君に恋文を送るのですが、姫君は返事を出しません。真木柱も継娘の中の姫君のことがあるので当惑するのでした。

The Rose Plum (*Kōbai*)

The wife of Kashiwagi's younger brother, Lord Inspector Kōbai, died leaving two daughters, the First Princess and the Middle Princess. Kōbai then married Makibashira, the daughter of Higekuro and widow of the late Prince Hotaru, and she bore him a son.

Makibashira also brought to her second marriage a daughter by Hotaru. Kōbai treated this stepdaughter as one of his own children but was also interested in just how pretty she might be. She, however, kept him at arm's length, vexing him by neither letting him see her when he visited or even hear her lute playing. He was privately worried that she might prove to be more beautiful than his own daughters.

He sent the First Princess to court as a consort of the Crown Prince. For the Middle Princess, he hoped to attract Prince Niou and tried to interest him in the match by sending him via his son, Taifu no Kimi, a fragrant branch of rose plum from his garden with a poem attached. But Niou did not respond to the overture, as he was taken instead with Makibashira's daughter by the late Prince Hotaru.

Prince Niou entrusted Taifu no Kimi with love letters to her, but she did not respond. Makibashira was in a difficult position, given that she herself was the Middle Princess's stepmother.

竹河 (*Takekawa*) Bamboo River

44 竹河

　鬚黒の大臣の死後、北の方の玉鬘は二人の美しい娘、大君と中の君の将来に頭を悩ませていました。

　今上帝や冷泉院からは大君を所望され、夕霧の息子の蔵人の少将も大君に求婚していました。玉鬘は、かつて自分も尚侍（天皇に近侍する内侍司の長官）となりながら、すぐに鬚黒と結婚してしまったこともあって、大君を冷泉院のもとへ差し上げようかと思うのですが、決めかねています。

　薫も、度々玉鬘の邸を訪れます。玉鬘は源氏を思い出して懐かしがり、不思議に亡き柏木に似ている薫を婿にしてみたいと思うのでした。

　桜の花盛りの頃、大君と中の君姉妹は、庭の桜を賭けて碁を打っていました。その姿を垣間見た蔵人の少将は、大君への思いを一層つのらせますが叶いません。

　結局、姉の大君は冷泉院に入り、翌年には姫君を出産しました。帝は、故鬚黒が姫君を入内させることを望んでいたにもかかわらず、院へ出仕させたことを不快に思います。玉鬘の三人の息子たちも、母への不満をあらわにするのでした。

　一方、妹の中の君は、母から尚侍の職を譲り受け、帝に仕えることになりました。

　数年後、大君は男君にも恵まれましたが、周囲の人々に妬まれ、里へ帰ることが多くなっていきました。

　さらに年が経ち、中納言になった薫が、昇進の挨拶に訪れたとき、玉鬘は薫に、大君のことを相談するのでした。

Bamboo River (*Takekawa*)

After the death of Higekuro, Tamakazura was greatly concerned about the future of their two daughters, the elder and younger princesses.

Both the current Emperor and Retired Emperor Reizei were interested in the elder, as was Kurōdo no Shōshō, a son of Yūgiri. Tamakazura's service as a Principal Handmaid to Reizei had been cut short by her marriage to Higekuro, and so she now thought that she might like to offer him the elder girl, but she could not make up her mind.

Kaoru, too, visited Tamakazura from time to time. Recalling Genji and thinking fondly of the past, she saw how much Kaoru resembled her dead half-brother Kashiwagi and thought she might like to have him as a son-in-law.

One day when the cherry blossoms were at their height, the two daughters were playing a game of *go*, with the cherry tree in the garden as the stakes. Catching a glimpse of them, Kurōdo no Shōshō was attracted to the elder girl all the more, but in vain.

She was sent instead into the service of Retired Emperor Reizei, and the next year gave birth to a daughter. The Emperor was vexed that despite the late Higekuro's hopes of sending her into his service, she had been presented to the Retired Emperor instead. Tamakazura's three sons also made no secret of their dissatisfaction with her decision.

It was the younger daughter who took over her mother's old position as a Principal Handmaid and went into the Emperor's service.

Several years later the elder girl was blessed with a son. But she was also the object of much jealousy on the part of her peers and frequently sought refuge at home.

Later still, during a visit by Kaoru on the occasion of his promotion to Middle Counselor, Tamakazura discussed with him her elder daughter's troubles.

橋姫 (*Hashihime*) The Princess at the Bridge

45 橋姫

その頃、源氏の異母弟にあたる八の宮は、宇治でひっそりと暮らしていました。かつては、源氏を憎く思っていた弘徽殿の大后に、皇位をめぐって東宮（後の冷泉帝）と兄弟で争わされ、源氏が政権に復帰してからは政界から見捨てられ、不遇の日を過ごしていました。北の方にも先立たれ、遺された大君と中の君の二人の姫君の養育のために出家も出来ず、在俗のまま仏道修行に励んでいました。邸までも火事で焼けてしまったため、娘たちとともに宇治の山荘に移り住みました。この八の宮の噂を聞いた薫は、仏道を学ぶために宇治へ通い始めます。

いつしか三年の月日が過ぎ、秋の末、八の宮が山寺に籠もっている留守に宇治を訪れた薫は、有明の月の光の下で、大君と中の君姉妹が琴と琵琶を合奏する姿を垣間見、大君に恋をしてしまいます。

その日、薫は、柏木の乳母子だと名乗る老女の弁から柏木の遺言を伝えたいと語られますが、人目を憚り、次の機会にと約束して帰京しました。

匂宮は薫から宇治の姫君たちのことを聞き、興味をもち、会いたいと思います。

十月、再び宇治を訪れた薫は、八の宮から姫君たちの後見を託されます。その明け方、薫は弁から、自分の出生の秘密を知らされ、柏木が死の床で女三の宮に宛てた手紙を手渡されます。実父の手紙を見て薫は衝撃を受けます。

しかし、帰京して母の女三の宮を訪れた薫は、尼宮がおっとりとお経を読んでいる姿を見て、秘密を知ったことを言い出せず、自分ひとりの胸のうちにおさめておこうと思うのでした。

The Princess at the Bridge (*Hashihime*)

Meanwhile, the Eighth Prince, a younger half-brother of Genji, had been living quietly in Uji. Long ago, Genji's old nemesis Junior Consort Kokiden had drawn him into a succession dispute with another half-brother, the Crown Prince (later Emperor Reizei). When Genji returned to power, the Eighth Prince had been passed over and faded into obscurity. His wife had also died, and so rather than take religious vows he had remained in the world to look after his two daughters, Ōigimi (Elder Princess) and Naka no Kimi (Middle Princess), while at the same time pursuing his Buddhist devotions. Then to make matters worse, his mansion burned to the ground, and he took his two daughters to live in his villa in Uji. Kaoru heard of him and began going there for Buddhist instruction.

Three years passed, and then late in autumn, Kaoru called at Uji when the Eighth Prince was in retreat in a mountain temple. By the light of the dawn moon, he caught a glimpse of Ōigimi and Naka no Kimi playing the *koto* and lute together, and he was smitten by the elder daughter. *play together → sisterly ♡*

Later that day, an old woman named Ben no Kimi, who introduced herself as Kashiwagi's foster sister (they had shared the same nurse as infants), told him that she had information about the late Kashiwagi to convey to him. But there were too many people about at the moment, and so after agreeing to call again, Kaoru returned to the capital.

There, he spoke of the ladies to Niou, pricking his friend's curiosity.

Kaoru went to Uji again in the tenth month, at which time the Eighth Prince put both the daughters under his care. Toward dawn, Ben no Kimi told Kaoru the secret of his birth and gave him a letter to his mother, the Third Princess, that Kashiwagi had written on his deathbed. Kaoru was deeply troubled to see the letter from his real father.

But when he called on his mother after returning to the capital, he found himself unable to speak to her of the secret as she sat so serenely reading her sutras. He decided to keep his knowledge to himself.

椎本 (*Shiigamoto*) Beneath the Oak

46 椎 本

　二月二十日過ぎ、薫から聞かされた宇治の姫君たちに関心を寄せる匂宮は、初瀬詣での帰り、夕霧の宇治の別邸に中宿りしました。対岸に八の宮の邸があることはもちろん知っていました。

　迎えに来た薫や公達と管絃の遊びをしていると、その音色を聞いた川向こうの八の宮から薫へ手紙が送られてきました。身分柄、軽々しく訪ねられない匂宮が返事を書き、薫はその手紙を届けに八の宮邸を訪れました。それ以来、匂宮から、姫君あての手紙が度々届くようになりました。八の宮はその返事を中の君にさせました。

　大君は二十五歳、中の君は二十三歳で、すでに婚期を逸している姫君たちの将来に、八の宮は胸を痛めているのでした。

　秋になり、中納言に昇進した薫が、宇治を訪れると、八の宮はその年が厄年にあたり、死期が近づいていることを感じ、いっそう勤行に励んでいるものの、自分がいなくなった後の姫君たちの行く末を案じて、再び薫に託すのでした。しかし一方で、八の宮は姫君たちに、軽はずみな結婚はしないように、とさとして、秋も深まった頃、山寺に参籠し、臨終を迎えました。

　八の宮の葬儀も追善供養も、すべて薫が手配しました。匂宮も弔問の手紙を度々届けるのでした。

　年の暮れ、薫は、雪の中を踏み分けて宇治を訪れ、大君に恋心を打ち明けますが、大君は受け入れません。

　年が明けて夏、宇治を訪れた薫は、喪服姿の美しい姉妹を垣間見、気品あふれる大君に一層心そそられるのでした。

Beneath the Oak (*Shiigamoto*)

After the twentieth of the second month, Niou returned from a pilgrimage from Hatsuse and had occasion to stay at a residence owned by his mother's half-brother Yūgiri in Uji on the way. He had heard of the two Uji ladies from Kaoru and knew that the Eighth Prince's villa lay just across the river.

Kaoru and other courtiers were in Prince Niou's suite, and as they amused themselves at pipes and strings, a note to Kaoru arrived from the Eighth Prince, who had heard the music wafting over the water. Prevented by protocol from paying an informal call himself on the Prince, Niou wrote a reply and had Kaoru deliver it. Thereafter Niou wrote from time to time to the two Princesses as well, and their father had the younger one respond.

Ōigimi was now twenty-five and Naka no Kimi, twenty-three, both already growing old for marriage. The Prince worried about them constantly.

That autumn, Kaoru, now a Middle Counselor, again called at Uji. The year had been prophesied as a dangerous one for the Eighth Prince and he, feeling that he had little time left, had redoubled his devotions. And yet he continued to fret over what would happen to his daughters after he was gone, and he again asked Kaoru to be sure and look after them. He was careful, however, also to admonish his daughters not to enter into hasty liaisons. And with that he secluded himself in a mountain temple where, as autumn deepened, he died.

Kaoru oversaw every detail of the Prince's funeral and memorial ceremonies. Niou, too, sent messages of condolence from time to time.

At the end of the year, Kaoru braved the snow to call at Uji and confess his feelings for the elder daughter Ōigimi, but she could not return them.

The next summer, once more at Uji, Kaoru caught a glimpse of the beautiful sisters in their mourning robes, and Ōigimi's elegance made his love for her deepen further still.

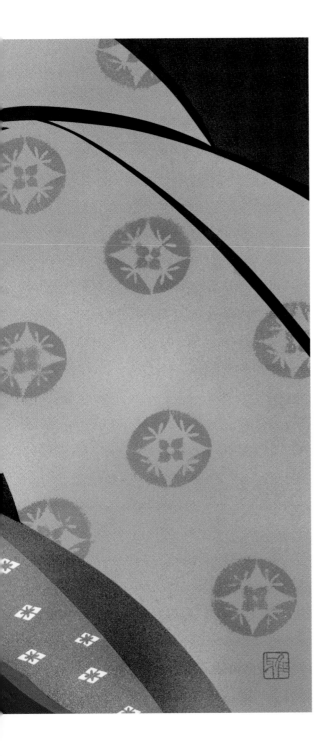

総角（*Agemaki*） Trefoil Knots

47 総角<ruby>総<rt>あげ</rt></ruby><ruby>角<rt>まき</rt></ruby>

八の宮の一周忌の準備に宇治を訪れた薫は、

> あげまきに長き契りを結びこめ
> おなじ所によりもあはなむ

〈名香の糸の総角結びに、永遠の契りを結びこめて、糸が同じ所に結び合わさるように、私といつまでも一緒にいて下さい。〉

と大君に再び胸中を訴えますが、この歌に対して大君は、

> ぬきもあへず涙の玉の緒に
> 長き契りをいかが結ばむ

〈緒に貫きとめられないほど、はかない涙の玉のような私の命ですのに、どうして永遠の契りを結べましょうか。〉

と詠み、薫の求愛を拒みます。

薫は弁に、故八の宮は自分に姫君たちのことを託されたのに、大君が強情にも断り続けるのは、いったいどうしたことかと相談します。弁は、大君は妹の中の君を、薫の相手に、と考えているらしいというのでした。薫は大君の寝所に入るものの、何ごともなく一夜を過ごしたのでした。

喪明けの頃、薫は弁の手引きで、二人の寝所に忍び込みますが、気配を察した大君は妹を残して抜け出してしまいました。薫は大君の仕打ちに腹立たしくも、中の君に手を出さず、物語などして夜を明かしたのでした。

薫は、こうなったら中の君を匂宮と結婚させようと考え、匂宮を宇治に案内し、匂宮と中の君は結ばれました。しかし大君は相変わらず薫を拒み続けます。

身分の高い匂宮にとって、宇治は遠く、なかなか来ることができません。十月、紅葉狩りに宇治まで来ていながら、中の君のもとに立ち寄れない匂宮に、姫君たちは落胆します。さらに、匂宮の夕霧の娘との縁談の噂に、妹の将来を案じる大君は、心労のあまりに病床に伏し、十一月、薫の看病もむなしく息を引き取ったのでした。

十二月、母の明石の中宮の許しを得て、匂宮は中の君を京に引き取る決心をします。

204

Trefoil Knots (*Agemaki*)

To prepare for the first anniversary of the death of the Eighth Prince, Kaoru called at Uji and again opened his heart to Ōigimi with a poem:

> Into this trefoil knot
> I braid
> my eternal vow
> that you and I
> will be likewise tied together.

She deflected him with this response:

> How could this cord of life,
> like teardrops
> no sooner strung than broken,
> be tied in vows
> for all eternity?

Kaoru then asked Ben no Kimi how Ōigimi could continue to reject his suit despite the Eighth Prince's having asked him to look out for both princesses. Ben no Kimi responded that she believed Ōigimi was actually hoping for a match between him and her younger sister. Kaoru nevertheless stole into Ōigimi's bedchamber, but he passed the night without making love with her.

The mourning period over, Kaoru enlisted Ben no Kimi's help in secreting him into the princesses' bedchamber, but Ōigimi sensed his presence and escaped, leaving Naka no Kimi behind. Angered by Ōigimi's behavior, Kaoru attempted no intimacy with the younger sister, instead talking the night away.

He then decided to arrange a marriage between Naka no Kimi and Niou, and to that end he invited his friend to Uji where Niou promptly seduced her. But Ōigimi nevertheless continued to reject Kaoru.

Niou's high rank constrained him from frequent visits to a place as distant as Uji. In the tenth month, he even went all the way to Uji to view the colored foliage but was not able to call on Naka no Kimi personally, to the disappointment of both princesses. There then came rumors in the bargain that he was to be betrothed to a daughter of Yūgiri. In despair about the future of her younger sister, Ōigimi took to her bed, and the next month, despite Kaoru's ministrations, she died.

In the last month of the year, Niou received permission from his mother, the Akashi Empress, and resolved to bring Naka no Kimi to the capital.

早蕨 (*Sawarabi*) Young Ferns

48 | 早蕨

　宇治にも春が訪れ、中の君のもとに、例年通り、山の阿闍梨（高僧）から蕨や土筆が届けられました。悲しみで面やつれした中の君に大君の面影を見る女房は、中の君が薫と縁のなかったことを残念がります。

　匂宮は二月初旬に、中の君を京の二条院に迎えることに決めました。薫は今更ながら、大君に似る中の君を匂宮に譲ったことを後悔しますが、支度に細かい心遣いをします。移転前日、宇治を訪れた薫と対面した中の君は、薫を見るにつけても、大君のことが改めて思い出され、胸に迫るものがあるのでした。その後、薫は弁の尼とこの世の無常について語り合いました。

　中の君は、上京の途中、宇治から京への道の険しさを目の当りにして、匂宮のたまさかの訪れを、少しだけ納得するのでした。

　その頃、夕霧の六の君の裳着の儀式が行われました。夕霧はこの姫君を匂宮と結婚させたかったのですが、中の君を京に迎えたことを知り、薫を婿にしたいと思い、話を持ちかけます。しかし薫はすげなく断るのでした。

　三月、二条院の匂宮を訪れた薫は、中の君とも話をします。匂宮は、薫と中の君との親しい関係に疑念をもつのでした。

Young Ferns (*Sawarabi*)

Spring finally came to Uji, and Naka no Kimi received the usual offering of ferns and mountain horsetails from a mountain ascetic, an old friend of the family. Seeing how Naka no Kimi's wasted face was coming to resemble that of the dead Ōigimi, her ladies-in-waiting regretted that she had not married Kaoru instead.

Niou decided to move her to his Nijō Mansion in the capital early in the second month. She so resembled her dead sister that Kaoru belatedly began to wish he had never given her away, but he nevertheless took great care in helping her prepare. On the day before the departure she had a meeting with Kaoru in Uji, and seeing him brought back wrenching memories of her sister. Afterward, Kaoru talked with the nun Ben no Kimi of the evanescence of life.

On her way to the capital, Naka no Kimi saw for herself how difficult the road to Uji was, and she began to understand why Niou's visits had been so infrequent.

This was also the time for the coming-of-age ceremony of Yūgiri's daughter, the Sixth Princess. Yūgiri had wanted to marry her to Niou, but on hearing that the young man was bringing Naka no Kimi to the capital, he decided instead to give her to Kaoru, and felt him out on the subject. But Kaoru flatly refused.

In the third month, Kaoru visited Niou at Nijō and also talked with Naka no Kimi, which made Niou suspect that there might be something between them.

宿木（*Yadorigi*）Mistletoe

49 | 宿木
やどり ぎ

　今上帝は、娘の女二の宮を薫に降嫁させたいと思い、碁の相
手に薫を召し、女二の宮との縁組みをほのめかします。薫は、
まだ大君のことが心に深く残っていたため、気が進まなかった
のですが、断りきれずに結婚を承諾したのでした。

　一方、このことを知った夕霧は、六の君の婿に匂宮を迎えよ
うと決意します。

　六の君と結婚した匂宮の訪れが遠のいた中の君は、嘆き悲し
み、宇治から上京したことを後悔するのでした。そんな中の君
に薫は同情し、慰めるうちに恋情をつのらせて迫り寄るのです
が、御懐妊のしるしの帯を見つけ、思いとどまったのでした。

　その後、中の君を訪れた匂宮は、中の君から薫の移り香がす
るのを不審に思い、中の君に問いただすものの、かえって情愛
がまさるのでした。

　ある日、中の君は、大君の人形を作って勤行に励みたいと語
る薫に、異母妹の浮舟の存在を告げます。秋、宇治を訪れた薫
は、弁の尼から浮舟の素性を聞きだし、仲介を頼みます。

　晩秋、匂宮は、中の君と薫との仲に疑惑を抱いていましたが、
琵琶を奏でる中の君の可愛らしさに、かえって愛情は深まって
いくばかりでした。翌年二月、中の君は男子を出産しました。
同じ頃、薫は、裳着をすませた女二の宮と結婚します。

　四月、薫は、宇治で偶然浮舟を垣間見て、亡き大君に似た美
しさに心動かされるのでした。

Mistletoe (*Yadorigi*)

The Emperor decided to give his daughter, the Second Princess, to Kaoru and summoned him for a game of *go*, at which time he hinted at the union. Kaoru, still mourning for Ōigimi, was not excited by the prospect, but he could not refuse the Emperor and acquiesced.

Hearing of this, Yūgiri decided to give his daughter, the Sixth Princess, to Niou.

After his marriage to the Sixth Princess, Niou's visits to Naka no Kimi became fewer, and she bitterly regretted ever having left Uji. Kaoru sympathized, and gradually his feelings turned to love. But on coming closer he caught sight of her maternity sash and abandoned his amorous notions.

Niou arrived thereafter and caught the suspicious scent of Kaoru's natural fragrance on his wife. He questioned her, but in the end found himself more in love than ever.

Kaoru one day told Naka no Kimi that he wanted to have a likeness made of Ōigimi and conduct religious services in her memory. Naka no Kimi then told him of her half-sister Ukifune (Drifting Boat). That autumn, Kaoru paid a call at Uji and questioned the nun Ben no Kimi about Ukifune's background, then asked her to serve as a go-between.

Toward the end of autumn, Niou again became suspicious of Naka no Kimi's relationship with Kaoru, but her loveliness as she played the lute rekindled in him deep feelings of love. In the second month of the following year, she gave birth to a boy. At the same time, the Second Princess had her coming-of-age ceremony and was married to Kaoru.

In the fourth month, Kaoru happened to catch a glimpse of Ukifune at Uji, and he was moved by her beauty, so like that of Ōigimi.

東屋（*Azumaya*）The Eastern Cottage

50 東屋

　薫の浮舟への関心を、弁の尼から聞いた浮舟の母の中将の君は、嬉しい反面、やはり身分相応の縁を、と考え、求婚者の中から、左近の少将を選びました。しかし少将は中将の君の夫、常陸の介の財力に目をつけていたため、浮舟が継子だと分かると破談にし、あげくには常陸の守の実子の姫君にのりかえました。母の中将の君はこの仕打ちに嘆き、浮舟を異母姉の中の君に預かってもらうことにしました。

　浮舟を連れて二条院に来た中将の君は、中の君とわが娘浮舟の境遇の違いを思い知らされ、匂宮や薫を目のあたりにして、夫とは全く比べものにならないほど美しく立派な二人に感動し、薫に娘を嫁がせることが出来ればと思うのでした。

　しかし、偶然、匂宮は自分の邸で浮舟を見つけ、中の君の妹とは知らずに言い寄ります。その場はかろうじて事なきを得ましたが、この出来事を聞いて驚いた中将の君は、浮舟を三条の小さな家に隠すことにしました。

　弁の尼からその事情を聞いた薫は、三条の隠れ家を訪れ、はじめて亡き大君の妹である浮舟に逢います。翌朝、浮舟を宇治に連れ去るのでした。

The Eastern Cottage (*Azumaya*)

Ukifune's mother, Chūjō no Kimi, learned from Ben no Kimi about Kaoru's feelings for her daughter, and though she was pleased, she felt a union with someone more equal in station would be preferable, and from among the various suitors chose Sakon no Shōshō, Lieutenant of the Left Guards. But the Lieutenant had his eyes on the fortune of the mother's second husband, the Vice Governor of Hitachi, and when he discovered that Ukifune was only his stepdaughter, he broke off the talks and began courting one of the Vice Governor's own daughters instead. Vexed, Ukifune's mother decided to have Ukifune live with her half-sister, Naka no Kimi.

Upon bringing her daughter to the Nijō Mansion, Chūjō no Kimi was struck by how much better Naka no Kimi's living situation was than her own daughter's, and she saw that her own husband paled by comparison to the handsome splendor of Niou and Kaoru. She resolved to do what she could to arrange a match between Kaoru and her daughter.

But Niou accidentally saw Ukifune in his mansion first, and not knowing she was Naka no Kimi's own younger half-sister, made advances. Ukifune barely managed to escape, and her shocked mother hid her in a small house in the Third Ward.

Kaoru learned of her whereabouts from Ben no Kimi and called at the Third Ward, where he saw the half-sister of his dead Ōigimi for the first time. The next morning, he took her to Uji.

浮舟（*Ukifune*）The Drifting Boat

51 | 浮 舟

匂宮は二条院で出逢った浮舟のことが、いまだに頭から離れませんでした。中の君は浮舟の素性を明かしませんでしたが、正月、宇治から中の君に届いた手紙を見て、匂宮は浮舟が宇治にいることを知ります。

その後、薫が浮舟を囲っていることをつきとめた匂宮は、宇治へ行き、薫を装って浮舟の部屋に入り、契ってしまいます。浮舟は匂宮と知り、あまりのことに呆然とし、中の君のことを思うにつけても申し訳なく、泣き崩れるのでした。匂宮は浮舟に夢中になり、翌日も宇治に留まり、愛し続けます。

しかし浮舟は、落ち着き払った薫とは対照的な、強引で情熱的に愛してくれる匂宮に、次第に惹かれていくのでした。

二月、久しぶりに宇治を訪れた薫は、浮舟が大人びていることを喜び、浮舟を京に迎えたいと話します。

薫の浮舟への思いを知った匂宮は焦り、雪深い中を宇治へ駆けつけ、浮舟を連れ出して、舟に乗せます。宇治川の対岸の隠れ家へ着くと、匂宮は自ら浮舟を抱いて舟から下ろし、隠れ家で耽溺の二日間を過ごすのでした。

その後、薫と匂宮の二人から、それぞれに京に迎えたいという手紙を受け取った浮舟は思い悩みます。

三月、薫と匂宮の文使いが、宇治で鉢合わせをしたことから、匂宮が浮舟のもとに通っていることを知った薫は、浮舟を責めます。

浮舟は、薫と匂宮との間にはさまれて悩み、思いつめたあげく、入水を決意するのでした。

The Drifting Boat (*Ukifune*)

Niou could not stop thinking about his meeting with Ukifune in the Nijō Mansion. Naka no Kimi did not tell him the girl's whole story, but after New Year's he saw a letter sent to Naka no Kimi from Uji and so discovered Ukifune's whereabouts.

Niou then ascertained that she was in Kaoru's care and so went to Uji, stole into her room disguised as Kaoru, and slept with her. Discovering that it was Niou, Ukifune was dumbfounded. Then guilty thoughts of Naka no Kimi made her collapse in tears. But Niou was head over heels, and he stayed at Uji the next day to be with her longer.

Ukifune gradually warmed to Niou's impetuous passion, so different from Kaoru's introspection and reserve.

In the second month, after a long absence, Kaoru again called at Uji and, happy to see how mature Ukifune had become, talked of bringing her to the capital.

Niou was stung when he learned of Kaoru's feelings toward Ukifune, and he raced through the deep snow to Uji. There he boarded a boat with her and crossed the river to a house where they could be alone. He lifted her from the boat himself, and they spent two intoxicating days together in their hideaway.

Ukifune thereafter received letters from both men announcing plans to take her to the capital, which threw her into emotional turmoil.

In the third month, messengers from both men encountered each other at Uji. As a result, Kaoru learned of Niou's visits and pressured Ukifune further.

Ukifune, torn between Kaoru and Niou, became increasingly distraught and finally decided to throw herself into the river.

蜻蛉（*Kagerō*）The Mayfly

52 蜻蛉
かげろう

　浮舟の突然の失踪に、宇治の邸は大騒ぎとなり、浮舟の母の
中将の君からも匂宮からも使いが寄越されました。浮舟の侍女
の右近は、昨夜浮舟が書いていた、中将の君あての手紙を読み、
入水の覚悟を知ります。

　中将の君も宇治に到着し、事の次第を知って泣き叫んで悲し
みますが、世間体を憚り、亡きがらのないまま、その夜、葬儀
を済ませてしまうのでした。

　その頃、薫は、母女三の宮の病気平癒の祈禱のため、石山寺
へ参籠していて、遅れて事態を知り、自分の運命のつたなさを
嘆くのでした。匂宮も二、三日正気を失うほど悲しみ、ついに
は病に臥してしまいます。薫はそんな匂宮の様子を見て、やは
り浮舟と密通していたと確信したのでした。

　その後、宇治を訪れた薫は、右近から入水前後の浮舟の様子
を聞き、四十九日の法要を手配し、遺族の面倒を見ることを約
束します。

　蓮の花盛りの頃、明石の中宮の法華八講の日、薫は正妻の姉
である女一の宮を垣間見て、その高貴な美しさに心惹かれるの
でした。妻の女二の宮に同じ格好をさせてみますが、姉宮とは
比べようもありません。それからは度々、女一の宮のもとに出
入りするようになります。

　薫はその邸で、女一の宮に宮仕えしている亡き式部卿の宮の
姫君と出会います。父が存命していれば、東宮妃にもなったか
もしれないほどの人です。薫は、姫君の身の上にこの世の無常
を思い、宇治に散った大君、浮舟を回想し、感慨をもよおさず
にはいられないのでした。

The Mayfly (*Kagerō*)

Ukifune's sudden disappearance caused an uproar at the Uji villa, and her mother Chūjō no Kimi and Niou both sent messengers. Reading a letter her mistress had written and addressed to her mother the night before, Ukifune's lady-in-waiting Ukon realized that she had planned to drown herself.

Chūjō no Kimi wept and wailed when she arrived in Uji and heard what had happened. Worried about appearances, they held a funeral service that night, though no body had been found.

Kaoru, meanwhile, had been on a pilgrimage to Ishiyama Temple to pray for the health of his mother, the Third Princess. When he belatedly heard the news about Ukifune, he railed against his own wretched fate. Niou was out of his mind for days, prostrate at the news. Seeing Niou's condition, Kaoru realized that his friend and Ukifune had indeed been lovers.

Thereafter Kaoru went to Uji and heard the story of Ukifune's drowning from Ukon. He took charge of the memorial ceremony for the forty-ninth day after death and promised to look after the people the lady had left behind.

When the lotus blossoms were at their height, the Akashi Empress commissioned a formal reading of the *Lotus Sutra*. During the event, Kaoru caught a glimpse of the First Princess, elder sister of his principal wife, and was struck by her regal beauty. He had his own wife, the Second Princess, put on identical garments, but there was still no comparison to her older sister. He began to visit the First Princess from time to time.

At the mansion of the First Princess, Kaoru met a daughter of Genji's younger half-brother, the late Prince Shikibu, the Minister of Rites, who was now in the Princess's service. Had the Prince lived, the daughter would now have been married to the Crown Prince. Struck by the vicissitudes of life that had brought her to this pass, Kaoru was led to reflect on the sad fates of Ōigimi and Ukifune at Uji.

手習 (*Tenarai*) Writing Practice

53 | 手習

　その頃、比叡山に横川の僧都という高僧がいました。春、その母尼と妹尼が初瀬詣でに行った帰り、母尼の具合が悪くなり、山籠もりをしていた僧都もそこに駆けつけ、一行は宇治の院に泊まることになりました。

　尼君たちより一足先に、院に出向いた僧都たちは、院の裏手の木の下で、茫然自失して泣いている女（浮舟）を発見します。

　浮舟を、亡き娘の身代わりと信じた妹尼は、懸命に介護し、小野に連れて帰ります。

　依然として回復しないまま、四月、五月が過ぎましたが、妹尼のたっての願いで下山した僧都の加持によって、ようやく正気を取り戻したのでした。しかし、浮舟は身元を明かそうとはせず、わが身を憂う歌などを手習いに綴るばかりなのでした。

　秋、小野を訪れた、妹尼の亡き娘の婿であった中将は浮舟を見かけて執拗に迫ります。浮舟は、男女のことから離れたいと思う気持ちがつのっていきます。

　そして九月、妹尼の留守の折、小野に立ち寄った僧都に懇願して、浮舟は出家を遂げたのでした。帰ってきた妹尼は、浮舟の尼姿を見てひどく悲しみますが、浮舟はようやく心の平安を得たような気がするのでした。

　僧都は、明石の中宮に浮舟のことを語ります。

　翌年、明石の中宮の女房を通じて、浮舟の生存を知らされた薫は、横川に行って、真相を確かめようと思うのでした。

Writing Practice (*Tenarai*)

The Bishop of Yokawa, an esteemed prelate, was at this time living on Mount Hiei. That spring his mother and younger sister, both nuns, were returning from a pilgrimage to Hatsuse when the mother fell ill. The Bishop hurried down from his mountain retreat, and it was arranged for the party to pause for a time at the Uji villa.

The Bishop arrived before the others, and beneath a tree at the back of the villa, he discovered a young lady dazed and weeping. It was Ukifune.

The Bishop's younger sister looked on Ukifune as a substitute for the daughter she herself had lost. She nursed her to the best of her ability and took her back to Ono.

When the fourth and fifth months passed with no improvement in Ukifune's condition, the younger nun implored her brother the Bishop to come down once more. Thanks to his rituals, Ukifune finally recovered her senses. But she refused to reveal her identity and spent her days writing out melancholy poems.

That autumn, a captain who had been the husband of the nun's dead daughter called at Ono. He discovered Ukifune and pursued her relentlessly, making Ukifune wish more than ever to be free once and for all from affairs of the heart.

In the ninth month, when the younger nun was away, Ukifune implored the Bishop, then in Ono, to administer holy orders, which he did. Upon her return, the nun was shocked and saddened to see the young lady in religious garb, but she also sensed that Ukifune had at last found peace.

The Bishop then spoke of Ukifune with the Akashi Empress.

Next year, Kaoru heard from one of the Empress's ladies-in-waiting that Ukifune was still alive. He went to Yokawa to learn if it was true.

夢浮橋（*Yume no ukihashi*）The Floating Bridge of Dreams

54 | 夢浮橋

薫は、浮舟の異父弟の小君を連れて横川の僧都を訪ね、浮舟が助けられてから出家するまでのいきさつを聞いて驚きます。

薫の呆然とした様子に、僧都は浮舟を早々と出家させてしまったことを後悔しますが、薫を浮舟のもとに案内することは断ります。そして、浮舟への手紙を小君に託しました。

その夜、横川から下山する薫一行の松明の灯りを見て、浮舟は念仏を唱えて気を紛らわすのでした。

薫は浮舟へ気持ちを伝えようと、小君に手紙を託して、再度小野へ向かわせます。僧都からの手紙には、薫の愛執の罪を晴らしてさしあげるように、とありました。そして、薫からの手紙には、

「罪深いあなたを、僧都に免じてお許しいたします。
　　法の師とたづぬる道をしるべにて
　　　思はぬ山にふみまどふかな
　　〈仏道の師として僧都を訪ねてきた、その道を道標にして、思いも寄らぬ恋の山に踏み迷っているなあ。〉
　小君のことをもうお忘れでしょうか。」

とありました。

しかし、弟の小君の来訪は、浮舟に母を思い出させましたが、以前と変わり果ててしまった尼姿を見られるのも恥ずかしく、また今の心の平静が乱れることを恐れた浮舟は、弟にも会わず、薫の手紙にも人違いだとして返事を書こうともしませんでした。

むなしく帰京した小君を迎えた薫は、浮舟が誰かに囲われているのではないかと疑いをもつのでした。

The Floating Bridge of Dreams (*Yume no ukihashi*)

Kaoru called on the Bishop of Yokawa in the company of a boy, Uki-fune's younger half-brother Kogimi, and was shocked when he learned that she was alive and had become a nun.

Seeing Kaoru's agitation, the Bishop regretted that he had so quickly acquiesced to Ukifune's request to take religious vows, but he neverthe-less refused to take Kaoru to her. He did, however, entrust Kogimi with a letter to her.

Seeing the torches of Kaoru's party as they returned down the moun-tain from Yokawa that night, Ukifune took refuge in chanting the holy name.

Hoping to convey his feelings, Kaoru wrote a letter and had it deliv-ered by Kogimi. In the Bishop's letter was an injunction to her to go back to Kaoru and thus dispel his sin of obsessive attachment. And in Kaoru's letter was this:

> Out of respect for the Bishop, I will forgive the sin you
> have committed.

> The road I took
> to find a teacher
> of the Good Law,
> has led me to lose my way
> on an unexpected mountain.

Have you completely forgotten your brother Kogimi?

But though Kogimi indeed recalled to mind her mother, Ukifune was embarrassed to be seen by him in her nun's habit, such a complete change from the past, and she was also afraid of losing her new-found tranquillity. She refused in the end to see her younger brother and returned the letter with no answer, saying that it was a case of mistaken identity.

When Kogimi returned empty-handed to the capital, Kaoru sus-pected that someone was hiding Ukifune from the world.

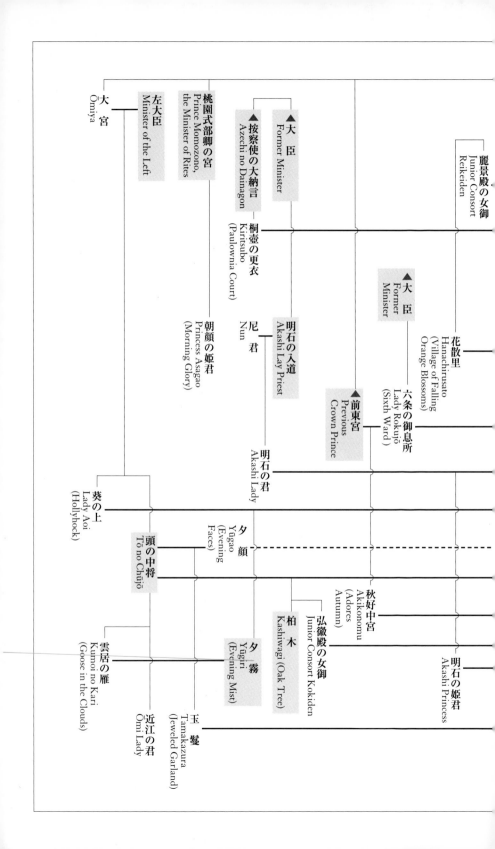

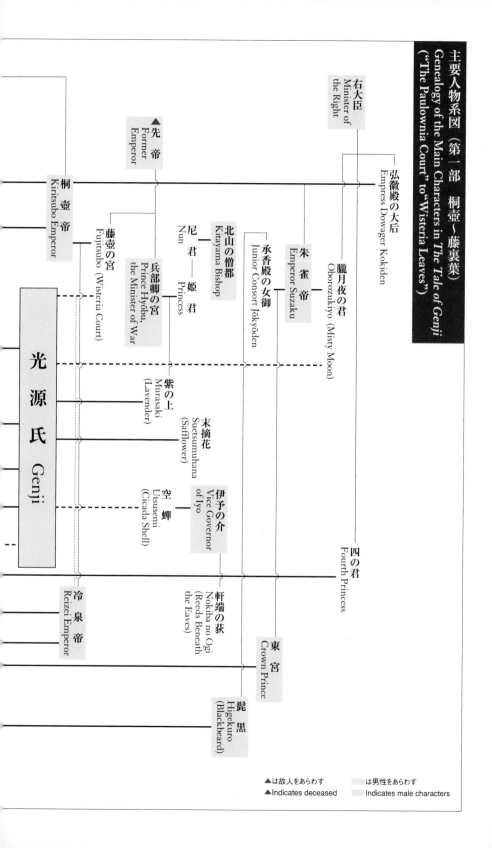

主要人物系図 （第一部 桐壺～藤裏葉）
Genealogy of the Main Characters in *The Tale of Genji*
("The Paulownia Court" to "Wisteria Leaves")

右大臣
Minister of
the Right

弘徽殿の大后
Empress Dowager Kokiden

▲先 帝
Former
Emperor

朱 雀 帝
Emperor Suzaku

朧月夜の君
Oborozukiyo (Misty Moon)

桐 壺 帝
Kiritsubo Emperor

藤壺の宮
Fujitsubo (Wisteria Court)

北山の僧都
Kitayama Bishop

尼 君
Nun

兵部卿の宮
Prince Hyōbu,
the Minister of War

姫 君
Princess

承香殿の女御
Junior Consort Jōkyōden

光 源 氏 Genji

紫の上
Murasaki
(Lavender)

末摘花
Suetsumuhana
(Safflower)

空 蟬
Utsusemi
(Cicada Shell)

伊予の介
Vice Governor
of Iyo

四の君
Fourth Princess

冷 泉 帝
Reizei Emperor

軒端の荻
Nokiba no Ogi
(Reeds Beneath
the Eaves)

東 宮
Crown Prince

髭 黒
Higekuro
(Blackbeard)

▲は故人をあらわす
▲Indicates deceased

は男性をあらわす
Indicates male characters

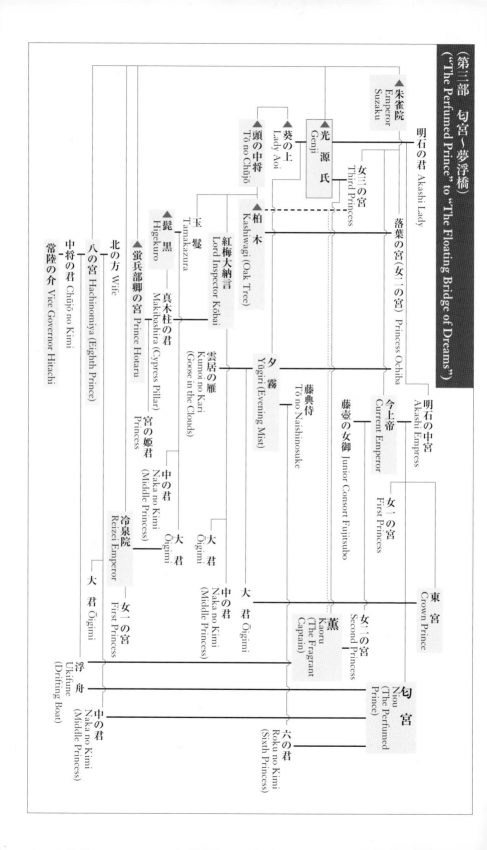

（第三部　匂宮～夢浮橋）
("The Perfumed Prince" to "The Floating Bridge of Dreams")

朱雀院 Emperor Suzaku

葵の上 Lady Aoi

光源氏 Genji

頭の中将 Tō no Chūjō

女三の宮 Third Princess

明石の君 Akashi Lady

落葉の宮（女二の宮）Princess Ochiba

柏木 Kashiwagi (Oak Tree)

玉鬘 Tamakazura

髭黒 Higekuro

紅梅大納言 Lord Inspector Kōbai

真木柱の君 Makibashira (Cypress Pillar)

蛍兵部卿の宮 Prince Hotaru

雲居の雁 Kumoi no Kari (Goose in the Clouds)

夕霧 Yūgiri (Evening Mist)

藤典侍 Tō no Naishinosuke

今上帝 Current Emperor

明石の中宮 Akashi Empress

藤壺の女御 Junior Consort Fujitsubo

女一の宮 First Princess

宮の姫君 Princess

北の方 Wife

八の宮 Hachinomiya (Eighth Prince)

中将の君 Chūjō no Kimi

常陸の介 Vice Governor Hitachi

中の君 Naka no Kimi (Middle Princess)

大君 Ōigimi

大君 Ōigimi

中の君 Naka no Kimi (Middle Princess)

冷泉院 Reizei Emperor

女一の宮 First Princess

大君 Ōigimi

大君 Ōigimi

中の君 Naka no Kimi (Middle Princess)

薫 Kaoru (The Fragrant Captain)

女二の宮 Second Princess

東宮 Crown Prince

匂宮 Niou (The Perfumed Prince)

大君 Ōigimi

浮舟 Ukifune (Drifting Boat)

中の君 Naka no Kimi (Middle Princess)

六の君 Roku no Kimi (Sixth Princess)

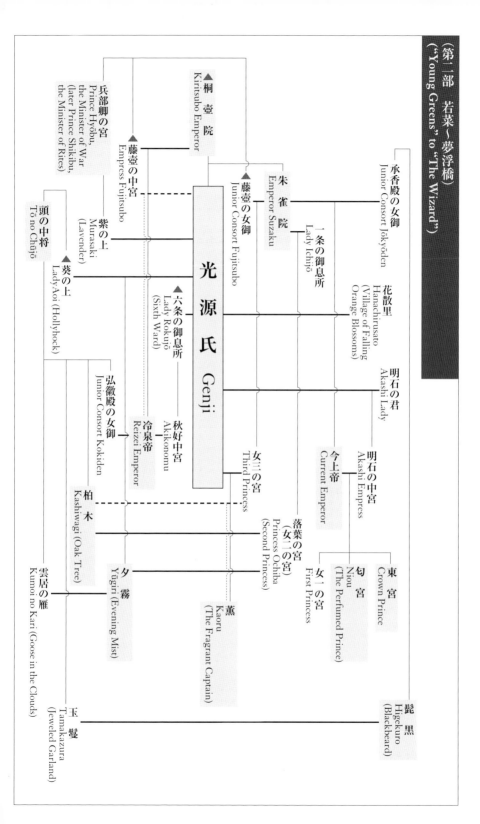

承香殿の女御
Junior Consort Jōkyōden

桐壺院
Kiritsubo Emperor

藤壺の中宮
Empress Fujitsubo

兵部卿の宮
Prince Hyōbu,
the Minister of War
(later Prince Shikibu,
the Minister of Rites)

朱雀院
Emperor Suzaku

藤壺の女御
Junior Consort Fujitsubo

一条の御息所
Lady Ichijō

花散里
Hanachirusato
(Village of Falling
Orange Blossoms)

明石の君
Akashi Lady

明石の中宮
Akashi Empress

今上帝
Current Emperor

東宮
Crown Prince

女一の宮
First Princess

匂宮
Niou
(The Perfumed Prince)

紫の上
Murasaki
(Lavender)

葵の上
Lady Aoi (Hollyhock)

頭の中将
Tō no Chūjō

光源氏
Genji

六条の御息所
Lady Rokujō
(Sixth Ward)

秋好中宮
Akikonomu

冷泉帝
Reizei Emperor

弘徽殿の女御
Junior Consort Kokiden

女三の宮
Third Princess

柏木
Kashiwagi (Oak Tree)

夕霧
Yūgiri (Evening Mist)

落葉の宮
（女二の宮）
Princess Ochiba
(Second Princess)

薫
Kaoru
(The Fragrant Captain)

雲居の雁
Kumoi no Kari (Goose in the Clouds)

髭黒
Higekuro
(Blackbeard)

玉鬘
Tamakazura
(Jeweled Garland)

略歴 ◆ CONTRIBUTOR'S PROFILES

宮田雅之
みやた まさゆき
Miyata Masayuki

切り絵画家。1926年東京生まれ。文豪谷崎潤一郎に見出され、独創の切り絵の世界を確立。一枚の紙を、一本の刀で切り上げる切り絵の技術と、その卓越した国際性を高く評価され、1981年、バチカン近代美術館に『日本のピエタ』が収蔵される。1995年、国連50周年を記念して、世界の現代画家の中から、日本人として初めて国連公認画家に選任され、力作『赤富士』が特別限定版画となって世界184ヵ国に紹介されるなど、切り絵界の第一人者として世界画壇で活躍。1997年1月5日、上海から帰国の途中急逝。代表作に『おくのほそ道』、『源氏物語』、『竹取物語』などがある。

瀬戸内寂聴
せとうち じゃくちょう
Setouchi Jakuchō

作家。徳島市生まれ。1943(昭18)東京女子大学卒業。1957(昭32)、『女子大生・曲愛玲』で第3回新潮社同人雑誌賞を受賞。1961(昭36)、伝記小説『田村俊子』で第1回田村俊子賞を受賞。1963(昭38)、『夏の終わり』で第2回女流文学賞を受賞。1974(昭48)中尊寺において得度受戒、法名寂聴。伝記小説『かの子撩乱』(昭65)、自伝小説『いずこより』など、女の業を書く作家の地位を確立。(平4)『花に問え』で谷崎潤一郎賞を受賞。1996(平8)、『白道』で芸術選奨文部大臣賞を受賞。1997(平9)、文化功労者に選ばれる。1998(平10)、NHK放送文化賞受賞。1998年4月、『源氏物語』全10巻を完結。

ドナルド・キーン
Donald Keene

日本文学研究者。コロンビア大学名誉教授。1922年ニューヨーク市生まれ。コロンビア大学で1951年に学位取得。ケンブリッジ大学、京都大学などでも日本文学を研究。1955年から1992年までコロンビア大学教授。現在、名誉教授に。

主な著書に『日本文学史』(1976年〜、9冊既刊)、『百代の過客』、『日本文学の歴史』(全18巻)などがある。また近松門左衛門、太宰治、三島由紀夫らの英訳も多数。

日本文学の国際的評価を高めるのに貢献し、1962年に菊池寛賞、75年に勲三等旭日綬章、83年に国際交流基金賞、98年に朝日賞などを受けている。

マック・ホートン
H. Mack Horton

カリフォルニア大学助教授、翻訳家。1952年ボストン生まれ。ハーバード大学で1981年に修士号取得。1989年、「日本古典文学」の研究でカリフォルニア大学バークレー校より博士号取得。ドナルド・キーンが初めて西洋に紹介した中世の連歌師、宗長が著した日記の翻訳、研究本(上下巻 スタンフォード大学出版会 2001年)を手がけ、その功績により、コロンビア大学のドナルド・キーン日本文化研究所より「1993—94日米友好委員会賞」を受賞。国立人文学財団(NEH)より奨学金を3回授与される。『源氏物語絵詞』(詞 瀬戸内寂聴 絵 石躍達哉 講談社 1999年)の英訳他、日本の文学、歴史、建築に関する翻訳多数。現在、『万葉集』(ハーバード大学出版会)の完訳を執筆中。

Paper cut-out illustrator. Born in Tokyo in 1926. He was discovered by the distinguished writer Tanizaki Jun'ichirō, and later went on to create his own distinct realm in *kiri-e* ("cut-out illustrations"). His cut-out pictures, made with mere sheets of paper and a cutting blade, have won admiration for their exceptional accessibility to people from all countries. In 1981, his work *Japanese Pietà* was selected for the modern religious art collection in the Vatican Museum. In 1995, the bicentennial anniversary of the United Nations, Miyata was selected from contemporary artists worldwide to be the United Nation's official artist, the first Japanese to hold the post. His masterpiece, *Red Fuji*, was reproduced in a special limited edition. Miyata continued to be actively engaged in international art circles until his death in 1997.

Miyata's representative works include illustrations for *The Narrow Road to Oku*, *The Tale of the Bamboo Cutter*, and *Love Songs from the Man'yōshū*.

Novelist. Born in Tokushima Prefecture in 1922. Graduated from Tokyo Christian Women's University. Setouchi started to write actively in the late 1950s, establishing her name with a biography of the pioneer feminist author Tamura Toshiko, which was awarded the first Tamura Toshiko Prize in 1961. She continued to write biographies of contemporary politicians and literary feminists and also published semiautobiographical novels. In 1973, she became a Buddhist nun.

Setouchi's principal works include the novel *Natsu no owari* (1962, The End of Summer) and *Kanoko ryōran* (serialized from 1962 to 1964; published in book form in 1971), a biographical novel of the contemporary woman write Okamoto Kanoko. She was named a "person of cultural merit" by the Japanese Ministry of Education in 1997. In 1998, she completed the modern Japanese translation of *The Tale of Genji*, and in the same year she won the NHK Broadcast Cultural Award.

U.S. scholar and translator of Japanese literature. Born in New York City in 1922. Keene graduated from Columbia University, where he received a Ph.D. in 1951 and taught from 1955 to 1992. He studied Japanese literature at Cambridge University, in England, and Kyoto University. His scholarly publications, ranging from a study of the *Kojiki* to discussions of contemporary literature, have established the foundations for the appreciation of Japanese literature in the West. Keene has been awarded the Kikuchi Kan Prize (1962), the Order of the Rising Sun (1974), the Japan Foundation Award (1984), and the Asahi Prize (1998) for his contribution to the study of Japanese literature.

His publications include *Travelers of a Hundred Ages* (1984), winner of the Yomiuri Literature Prize and the Shinchō Grand Prize; a four-volume history of Japanese literature— *Seeds in the Heart* (1993), *Dawn to the West* (two volumes, 1984), *World Within Walls* (1976)—as well as numerous translations.

U.S. scholar and translator. Born in Boston in 1952. Horton received an M.A. from Harvard University in 1981 and a Ph.D. in Japanese literature from the University of California, Berkeley, in 1989, where he is now Associate Professor. His publications include a two-volume translation and study of the poetic diary of Sōchō, a medieval linked-verse poet first introduced to Western readers by Donald Keene. That translation (Stanford University Press, 2001) won the 1993–94 Japan–U.S. Friendship Commission Prize for the Translation of Japanese Literature, awarded by the Donald Keene Center of Japanese Culture at Columbia. The recipient of three National Endowment for the Humanities grants, Horton has also translated *The Tale of Genji Picture Book* by Setouchi Jakuchō and Ishiodori Tatsuya (Kodansha, 1999) as well as numerous other works on Japanese literature, history, and architecture. He is currently producing for Harvard a complete translation of *Man'yōshū*.

源氏物語（げんじものがたり）
The Tale of Genji

2001年10月26日　第1刷発行

切り絵　宮田雅之（みやたまさゆき）
序　文　瀬戸内寂聴（せとうちじゃくちょう）
エッセイ　ドナルド・キーン
英　訳　マック・ホートン
本文協力　渡邊綾子
和文監修　高木和子（関西学院大学専任講師）
監修協力　村口進介（神戸大学大学院）
企画協力　宮田雅之アートプロモーション
株式会社雅房・瀧愁麗
発行者　野間佐和子
発行所　講談社インターナショナル株式会社
〒112-8652 東京都文京区音羽1-17-14
電話　03-3944-6493（編集部）
03-3944-6492（業務部・営業部）
ホームページ　http://www.kodansha-intl.co.jp
印刷所　光村印刷株式会社
製本所　株式会社 堅省堂

定価はカバーに表示してあります。

Printed in Japan.
ISBN 4-7700-2772-9